Night of the Millennium

Ruskin Bond is known for his signature simplistic and witty writing style. He is the author of several bestselling short stories, novellas, collections, essays and children's books; and has contributed a number of poems and articles to various magazines and anthologies. At the age of twenty-three, he won the prestigious John Llewellyn Rhys Prize for his first novel, *The Room on the Roof*. He was also the recipient of the Padma Shri in 1999, Lifetime Achievement Award by the Delhi Government in 2012, and the Padma Bhushan in 2014.

Born in 1934, Ruskin Bond grew up in Jamnagar, Shimla, New Delhi and Dehradun. Apart from three years in the UK, he has spent all his life in India, and now lives in Landour, Mussoorie, with his adopted family.

GW00544268

Night of the Millennium

Selected and Compiled by

RUSKIN BOND

RUPA

Published by
Rupa Publications India Pvt. Ltd 2019
7/16, Ansari Road, Daryaganj
New Delhi 110002

Sales centres:
Allahabad Bengaluru Chennai
Hyderabad Jaipur Kathmandu
Kolkata Mumbai

ISBN: 978-93-5333-522-9

First impression 2019

10 9 8 7 6 5 4 3 2 1

Printed at HT Media Ltd, Gr. Noida

CONTENTS

INTRODUCTION

In the last few weeks, I have been rummaging through my archives and fishing out a new set of stories—a compilation of chilling tales.

In this collection, you will find stories that are replete with terror, adventure, perils and thrills. Myriad themes run through them—the nightmarish, the uncanny, the mysterious and the unknown. Written by the masters of the genre the world over, these tales of horror have an international flavour that will cater to our affinities for the ghostly, supernatural elements around us.

Each story in this collection conveys a sense of the spooky and the paranormal. These unforgettable tales of human and superhuman encounters will be a treat for readers. And to enjoy them to the fullest, take this horror fan's advice—dive under the covers and read these gripping narratives, preferably late at night. Writers such as Saki, Rudyard Kipling, C.A. Kincaid, Bram Stoker, Alice Perrin, W.F. Harvey, Stacy Aumonier, H.P. Lovecraft and W.W. Jacobs will surely cast their magical spell on you.

Happy hauntings!

Ruskin Bond

NIGHT OF THE MILLENNIUM

Ruskin Bond

Jackals howled dismally, foraging for bones and offal down in the khud below the butcher's shop. Pasand was unperturbed by the sound. A robust young computer whiz-kid and patriotic multinational, he prided himself on being above and beyond all superstitious fears of the unknown. In his lexicon, the unknown was just something that was waiting to be discovered. Hence this walk, past the old cemetery late at night.

Midnight would see the new millennium in. The year 2000 beckoned, full of bright prospects for well-heeled young men like Pasand. True, there were millions—soon to be over a billion—sweating it out in the heat and dust of the plains below, scraping together a meagre living for themselves and their sprawling families. Not for them the advantages of a public school education, three cars in the garage, and a bank account in Bermuda. Ah well, mused Pasand, not everyone could have the brains and good luck, as well as inherited family wealth of course, that had made life so pleasant and promising for him. This was going to be the century in which the smart-asses would get to the top and all other varieties of asses would sink to the bottom. It was important to have a ruling elite, according to his philosophy; only then could slaves prosper!

He looked at his watch. It was just past midnight. He had eaten well, and he was enjoying his little walk along the lonely winding road which took him past the houses of the rich and famous, the Lais, the Banerjees, the Kapoors, the Ramchandanis— he was as good as any of them! Better, in fact. He was approaching his own personal Everest, while they had reached theirs and were on the downward slope, or so he presumed.

Here was the cemetery with its broken old tombstones, some of them dating from a hundred and fifty years ago: pathetic reminders of a once-powerful empire, now reduced to dust and crumbling monuments. Here lay colonels and magistrates, merchants and memsahibs, and many small children; fragile lives which had been snuffed out in more turbulent times. To Pasand, they were losers, all of them. He had nothing but contempt for those who hadn't been able to hang on to their power and glory. No lost empires for him!

The road here was very dark, for the trees grew thick on the northern slopes. Pasand felt a twinge of nervousness, but he was reassured by the feel of the cell phone in his pocket—he could always summon his driver or his armed bodyguard to come and pick him up.

The moon had risen over Nag Tibba, and the graves stood out in serried rows, as though forming a guard of honour for this modern knight in t-shirt and designer jeans. Through the deodars he saw a faint light on the perimeter of the cemetery. Here, he had learnt from one of his chamchas, lived a widow with a brood of small children. Although in poor health, she was still young and comely, and known to be lavish with her favours to those who were generous with their purses; for she needed the money for her hungry family.

She was also a little mad, they said, and preferred to sleep in one of the old domed tombs rather than in the quarters provided for her late husband, who had been the caretaker.

This did not bother Pasand. He was in search of sensual pleasure, not romance. And right now he felt an urgent need to exert his dominance over someone, preferably a woman, for he had to prove his manhood in some way. So far, most young women had shied away from his vainglorious and clumsy approach.

This woman wasn't young. She was in her late thirties, and poverty, malnutrition and ill-use had made her look much older. But there were vestiges of beauty in her smouldering eyes and sinewy limbs. Her gypsy blood must have had something to do with it. Her teeth gleamed in the darkness as she smiled at Pasand and invited him into her boudoir—the spacious tomb that she favoured most.

Pasand had no time for tender love-play. Clumsily, he clawed at her breasts but found they were not much larger than his own. He tore at her already tattered clothes, pressed his mouth hungrily to her dry lips. She made no attempt to resist. He had his way. Then, while he lay supine across the cold damp slab of a grave that covered the remains of some long-dead warrior, she leaned over him and bit him on the cheek and neck.

He cried out in pain and astonishment, and tried to sit up. But a number of hands, small but strong, thrust him back against the tombstone. Small mouths, sharp teeth, pressed against his flesh. Muddy fingers tore at his clothes. Those young teeth bit— and bit again. His screams mingled with the cries of the jackals.

'Patience, my children, patience,' crooned the woman. 'There is more than enough for all of you.'

They feasted.

Down in the ravine, the jackals started howling again, awaiting their turn. The bones would be theirs. Only the cell phone would be rejected.

THE DOCTOR'S GHOST

Dr Norman Macleod

A friend of mine, a medical man, once went on a fishing expedition with an old college acquaintance, an army surgeon, whom he had not met for many years, from his having been in India with his regiment. McDonald, the army surgeon, was a thorough Highlander, and slightly tinged with what is called the superstition of his countrymen, and at the time I speak of, was liable to rather depressed spirits from an unsound liver. His native air was, however, rapidly renewing his youth; and when he and his old friend paced along the banks of the fishing stream in a lonely part of Argyllshire, and sent their lines like airy gossamers over the pools, and touched the water over a salmon's nose, so temptingly that the best-principled and wisest fish could not resist the bite, McDonald had apparently regained all his buoyancy of spirit.

They had been fishing together for about a week with great success, when McDonald proposed to pay a visit to a family with which he was acquainted, that would separate him from his friend for some days. But whenever he spoke of their intended separation, he sank down into his old gloomy state, at one time declaring that he felt as if they were never to meet again.

My friend tried to rally him, but in vain. They parted at the trouting stream, McDonald's route being across a mountain pass, with which, however, he had been well acquainted in his youth, though the road was lonely and wild in the extreme.

The doctor returned early in the evening to his resting-place, which was a shepherd's house lying on the very outskirts of the 'settlements,' and beside a foaming mountain stream. The shepherd's only attendants at the time were two herd lads and three dogs. Attached to the hut, and communicating with it by a short passage, was rather a comfortable room which 'the Laird' had fitted up to serve as a sort of lodge for himself in the midst of his shooting-ground, and which he had put for a fortnight at the disposal of my friend.

Shortly after sunset on the day I mention, the wind began to rise suddenly to a gale, the rain descended in torrents, and the night became extremely dark. The shepherd seemed uneasy, and several times went to the door to inspect the weather. At last he roused the fears of the doctor for McDonald's safety, by expressing the hope that by this time he was 'owre that awfu' black moss, and across the red burn.'

Every traveller in the Highlands knows how rapidly these mountain streams rise, and how confusing the moor becomes in a dark night. The confusion of memory once a doubt is suggested, the utter mystery of places, becomes, as I know from experience, quite indescribable.

'The black moss and red burn' were words that were never after forgot by the doctor, from the strange feelings they produced when first heard that night; for there came into his mind terrible thoughts and forebodings about poor McDonald, and reproaches for never having considered his possible danger in attempting such a journey alone. In vain the shepherd assured him that he must have reached a place of safety before the darkness and the storm came on. A presentiment which he could not cast off made him so miserable that he could hardly refrain from tears. But nothing could be done to relieve the anxiety now become so painful.

The doctor at last retired to bed about midnight. For a long time he could not sleep. The raging of the stream below the small window, and the thuds of the storm, made him feverish and restless. But at last he fell into a sound and dreamless sleep. Out of this, however, he was suddenly roused by a peculiar noise in his room, not very loud, but utterly indescribable. He heard tap, tap, tap at the window, and he knew, from the relation which the wall of the room bore to the rock, that the glass could not be touched by human hand.

After listening for a moment, and forcing himself to smile at his nervousness, he turned round, and began again to seek repose. But now a noise began too near and loud to make sleep possible. Starting and sitting up in bed, he heard repeated in rapid succession, as if someone was spitting in anger, and close to his bed,—'Fit! Fit! Fit!' and then a prolonged 'whir-r-r' from another part of the room, while every chair began to move, and the table to jerk!

The doctor remained in breathless silence, with every faculty intensely acute. He frankly confessed that he heard his heart beating, for the sound was so unearthly, so horrible, and something seemed to come so near him, that he began seriously to consider whether or not he had some attack of fever which affected his brain—for, remember, he had not tasted a drop of the shepherd's small store of whisky! He felt his pulse, composed his spirits, and compelled himself to exercise calm judgment. Straining his eyes to discover anything, he plainly saw at last a white object moving, but without sound, before him. He knew that the door was shut and the window also.

An overpowering conviction then seized him, which he could not resist, that his friend McDonald was dead! By an effort he seized a lucifer-box on a chair beside him, and struck a light. No white object could be seen. The room appeared to be as when he went to bed. The door was shut. He looked at his watch, and particularly marked that the hour was twenty-two minutes past three. But the match was hardly extinguished when, louder than ever, the same unearthly cry of 'Fit! Fit! Fit!' was heard, followed by the same horrible whir-r-r-r, which made his teeth chatter. Then the movement of the table and every chair in the room was resumed with increased violence, while the tapping on the window was heard above the storm. There was no bell in the room, but the doctor, on hearing all this frightful confusion of sounds again repeated, and beholding the white object moving towards him in terrible silence, began to thump the wooden partition and to shout at the top of his voice for the shepherd, and having done so, he dived his head under the blankets!

The shepherd soon made his appearance, in his night-shirt, with a small oil-lamp, or 'crusey,' over his head, anxiously inquiring as he entered the room:

'What is't, doctor? What's wrang? Pity me, are ye ill?'

'Very!' cried the doctor. But before he could give any explanation a loud whir-r-r was heard, with the old cry of 'Fit!' close to the shepherd, while two chairs fell at his feet! The shepherd sprang back, with a half scream of terror the lamp was dashed to the ground, and the door violently shut.

'Come back!' shouted the doctor. 'Come back, Duncan, instantly, I command you!'

The shepherd opened the door very partially, and said, in terrified accents:

'Gude be aboot us, that was awfu'! What under heaven is't?'

'Heaven knows, Duncan,' ejaculated the doctor with agitated voice, 'but do pick up the lamp, and I shall strike a light.'

Duncan did so in no small fear; but as he made his way to the bed in the darkness to get a match from the doctor, something caught his foot; he fell; and then, amidst the same noises and tumults of chairs, which immediately filled the apartment, the 'Fit! Fit! Fit! Fit!' was prolonged with more vehemence than ever!

The doctor sprang up, and made his way out of the room, but his feet were several times tripped by some unknown power, so that he had the greatest difficulty in reaching the door without a fall. He was followed by Duncan, and both rushed out of the room, shutting the door after them. A new light having been obtained, they both returned with extreme caution, and, it must be added, real fear, in the hope of finding some cause or other for all those terrifying signs.

Would it surprise our readers to hear that they searched the room in vain?—that, after minutely examining under the table, chairs, bed, everywhere, and with the door shut, not a trace could be found of anything? Would they believe that they heard during the day how poor McDonald had staggered, half dead from fatigue, into his friend's house, and falling into a fit, had died at *twenty-two minutes past three* that morning? We do not ask anyone to accept of all this as true. But we pledge our honour to the following facts:

The doctor, after the day's fishing was over, had packed his rod so as to take it into his bedroom; but he had left a minnow attached to the hook. A white cat left in the room swallowed the minnow and was hooked. The unfortunate gourmand had vehemently protested against this intrusion into its upper lip by the violent 'Fit! Fit! Fit!' with which she tried to spit the hook out; the reel added the mysterious whir-r-r-r; and the disengaged line, getting entangled in the legs of the chairs and table, as the hooked cat attempted to flee from her tormentor, set the furniture in motion, and tripped up both shepherd and doctor; while an ivy branch kept tapping at the window! Will anyone doubt the existence of ghosts and a spirit-world after this?

I have only to add that the doctor's skill was employed during the night in cutting the hook out of the cat's lip, while his poor patient, yet most impatient, was held by the shepherd in a bag, the head alone of the puss, with hook and minnow, being visible. McDonald made his appearance in a day or two, rejoicing once more to see his friend, and greatly enjoying the ghost story.

THE PHANTOM 'RICKSHAW

Rudyard Kipling

May no ill dreams disturb my rest,
Nor Powers of Darkness me molest.

—Evening Hymn

One of the few advantages that India has over England is a great knowability. After five years' service a man is directly or indirectly acquainted with the two or three hundred civilians in his province, all the messes of ten or twelve regiments and batteries, and some fifteen hundred other people of the non-official caste. In ten years his knowledge should be doubled, and at the end of twenty he knows, or knows something about, every Englishman in the Empire, and may travel anywhere and everywhere without paying hotel bills.

Globetrotters who expect entertainment as a right, have, even within my memory, blunted this open-heartedness, but nonetheless today, if you belong to the Inner Circle and are neither a Bear nor a Black Sheep, all houses are open to you, and our small world is very, very kind and helpful.

Rickett of Kamartha stayed with Polder of Kumaon some

fifteen years ago. He meant to stay two nights, but was knocked down by rheumatic fever, and for six weeks disorganized Polder's establishment, stopped Polder's work, and nearly died in Polder's bedroom. Polder behaves as though he had been placed under eternal obligation by Rickett, and yearly sends the little Ricketts a box of presents and toys. It is the same everywhere. The men who do not take the trouble to conceal from you their opinion that you are an incompetent ass, and the women who blacken your character and misunderstand your wife's amusements, will work themselves to the bone on your behalf if you fall sick or into serious trouble.

Heatherlegh, the doctor, kept, in addition to his regular practice, a hospital on his private account—an arrangement of loose boxes for incurables, his friend called it—but it was really a sort of fitting-up shed for craft that had been damaged by the stress of weather. The weather in India is often sultry, and since the tale of bricks is always a fixed quantity, and the only liberty allowed is permission to work overtime and get no thanks, men occasionally break down and become as mixed as the metaphors in this sentence.

Heatherlegh is the dearest doctor that ever was, and his invariable prescription to all his patients is, 'Lie low, go slow, and keep cool.' He says that more men are killed by overwork than the importance of this world justifies. He maintains that overwork slew Pansay, who died under his hands about three years ago. He has, of course, the right to speak authoritatively, and he laughs at my theory that there was a crack in Pansay's head and a little bit of the Dark World came through and pressed him to death. 'Pansay went off the handle,' says Heatherlegh, 'after the stimulus of long leave at Home. He may or he may not have behaved like a blackguard to Mrs Keith-Wessington. My notion is that the work of the Katabundi Settlement ran him off his legs, and that he took to brooding and making much of an ordinary E & O flirtation. He certainly was engaged to Miss Mannering, and she certainly broke off the engagement. Then he took a feverish chill and all that nonsense about ghosts developed. Overwork started his illness, kept it alight, and killed him, poor devil. Write him off to the system that uses one man to do the work of two and a half men.'

I do not believe this. I use to sit up with Pansay sometimes when Heatherlegh was called out to patients and I happened to be within claim. The man would make me most unhappy by describing in a low, even voice, the procession that was always passing at the bottom of the bed. He had a sick man's command of language. When he recovered I suggested that he should write out the whole affair from beginning to end, knowing that this might assist him to ease his mind.

He was in a high fever while he was writing, and the blood-and-thunder magazine diction he adopted did not calm him. Two months afterwards he was reported fit for duty, but, in spite of the fact that he was urgently needed to help an undermanned commission stagger through a deficit, he preferred to die; vowing at the last that he was hag-ridden. I got his manuscript before he died, and this is his version of the affair, dated 1885, exactly as he wrote it:

My doctor tells me that I need rest and change of air. It is not improbable that I shall get both ere long—rest that neither the red-coated messenger nor the midday gun can break, and change of air far beyond that which any homeward-bound steamer can give me. In the meantime I am resolved to stay where I am; and, in flat defiance of my doctor's orders, to take all the world into my confidence. You shall learn for yourselves the precise nature of my malady, and shall, too, judge for yourselves whether any man born of woman on this weary earth was ever so tormented as I.

Speaking now as a condemned criminal might speak ere the drop-bolts are drawn, my story, wild and hideously improbable as it may appear, demands at least attention. That it will ever receive credence I utterly disbelieve. Two months ago I should have scouted as mad or drunk the man who had dared tell me the like. Two months ago I was the happiest man in India. Today, from Peshawar to the sea, there is no one more wretched. My doctor and I are the only two who know this. His explanation is, that my brain, digestion and eyesight are all slightly affected; giving rise to my frequent and persistent 'delusions'. Delusions, indeed! I call him a fool; but he attends me still with the same unwearied smile, the same bland professional manner, the same neatly-trimmed red whiskers, till I begin to suspect that I am an ungrateful, evil-tempered invalid. But you shall judge for yourselves.

Three years ago it was my fortune—my great misfortune—to sail from Gravesend to Bombay, on return from a long leave, with one Agnes Keith-Wessington, wife of an officer on the Bombay side. It does not in the least concern you to know what manner of woman she was. Be content with the knowledge that, ere the voyage had ended, both she and I were desperately and unreasoningly in love with one another. Heaven knows that I can make the admission now without one particle of vanity. In matters of this sort there is always one who gives and another who accepts. From the first day of our ill-omened attachment, I was conscious that Agnes's passion was stronger, more dominant, and—if I may use the expression—a purer sentiment than mine. Whether she recognized the fact then, I do not know. Afterwards it was bitterly plain to both of us.

Arrived at Bombay in the spring of the year, we went our respective ways, to meet no more for the next three or four months, when my leave and her love took us both to Simla. There we spent the season together; and there my fire of straw burnt itself out to a pitiful end with the closing year. I attempt no excuse. I make no apology. Mrs Wessington had given up much for my sake, and was prepared to give up all. From my own lips, in August 1882, she learnt that I was sick of her presence, tired of her company, and weary of the sound of her voice. Ninety-nine women out of a hundred would have wearied of me as I wearied of them; seventy-five of that number would have promptly avenged themselves by active and obtrusive flirtation with other men. Mrs Wessington was the hundredth. On her, neither my openly-expressed aversion nor the cutting brutalities with which I garnished our interviews had the least effect.

'Jack, darling!' was her one eternal cuckoo cry. 'I'm sure it's all a mistake—a hideous mistake; and we'll be good friends again some day. *Please* forgive me, Jack, dear.'

I was the offender, and I knew it. That knowledge transformed my pity into passive endurance, and, eventually, into blind hate—the same instinct, I suppose, which prompts a man to savagely stamp on the spider he has but half-killed. And with this hate in my bosom the season of 1882 came to an end.

Next year we met again at Simla—she with her monotonous face and timid attempts at reconciliation, and I with loathing of her in every fibre of my frame. Several times I could not avoid meeting her alone; and on each occasion her words were identically the same. Still the unreasoning wail that it was all a 'mistake'; and still the hope of eventually 'making friends'. I might have seen, had I cared to look, that that hope only was keeping her alive. She grew more wan and thin, month by month. You will agree with me, at least, that such conduct would have driven anyone to despair. It was uncalled for; childish; unwomanly. I maintain that she was much to blame.

And again, sometimes, in the black, fever-stricken night-watches, I have begun to think that I might have been a little kinder to her. But that really *is* a 'delusion'. I could not have continued pretending to love her when I didn't; could I? It would have been unfair to us both.

Last year we met again—on the same terms as before. The same weary appeals, and the same curt answers from my lips. At least I would make her see how wholly wrong and hopeless were her attempts at resuming the old relationship. As the season wore on, we fell apart—that is to say, she found it difficult to meet me, for I had other and more absorbing interests to attend to. When I think it over quietly in my sickroom, the season of 1884 seems a confused nightmare wherein light and shade were fantastically intermingled—my courtship of little Kitty Mannering; my hopes, doubts, and fears; our long rides together; my trembling avowal of attachment; her reply; and now and again a vision of a white face flitting by in the 'rickshaw with the black and white liveries I once watched for so earnestly; the wave of Mrs Wessington's gloved hand; and, when she met me alone, which was but seldom, the irksome monotony of her appeal. I loved Kitty Mannering; honestly, heartily loved her, and with my love for her grew my hatred for Agnes. In August, Kitty and I were engaged. The next day I met those accursed 'magpie' jhampanies at the back of Jakko, and, moved by some passing sentiment of pity, stopped to tell Mrs Wessington everything. She knew it already.

'So I hear you're engaged, Jack dear.' Then, without a moment's pause: 'I'm sure it's all a mistake—a hideous mistake. We shall be as good friends some day, Jack, as we ever were.'

My answer might have made even a man wince. It cut the dying woman before me like the blow of a whip. 'Please forgive me, Jack; I didn't mean to make you angry; but it's true, it's true!'

And Mrs Wessington broke down completely. I turned away and left her to finish her journey in peace, feeling, but only for a moment or two, that I had been an unutterably mean hound. I looked back, and saw that she had turned her 'rickshaw with the idea, I suppose, of overtaking me.

The scene and its surroundings were photographed on my memory. The rain-swept sky (we were at the end of the wet weather), the sodden, dingy pines, the muddy road, and the black powder-riven cliffs formed a gloomy background against which the black and white liveries of the jhampanies, the yellow-panelled 'rickshaw and Mrs Wessington's down-bowed golden head stood out clearly. She was holding her handkerchief in her left hand and was leaning back exhausted against the 'rickshaw cushions. I turned my horse up a bypath near the Sanjowlie Reservoir and literally ran away. Once I fancied I heard a faint call of 'Jack!'. This may have been imagination. I never stopped to verify it. Ten minutes later I came across Kitty on horseback; and, in the delight of a long ride with her, forgot all about the interview.

A week later Mrs Wessington died, and the inexpressible burden of her existence was removed from my life. I went Plainsward perfectly happy. Before three months were over I had forgotten all about her, except that at times the discovery of some of her old letters reminded me unpleasantly of our bygone relationship. By January, I had disinterred what was left of our correspondence from among my scattered belongings and had burnt it. At the beginning of April of this year, 1885, I was at Simla—semi-deserted Simla—once more, and was deep in lover's talks and walks with Kitty. It was decided that we should be married at the end of June. You will understand, therefore, that, loving Kitty as I did, I am not saying too much when

I pronounce myself to have been, at that time, the happiest man in India.

Fourteen delightful days passed almost before I noticed their flight. Then, aroused to the sense of what was proper among mortals, circumstanced as we were, I pointed out to Kitty that an engagement ring was the outward and visible sign of her dignity as an engaged girl; and that she must forthwith come to Hamilton's to be measured for one. Up to that moment, I give you my word, we had completely forgotten so trivial a matter. To Hamilton's we accordingly went on 15 April 1885. Remember that—whatever my doctor may say to the contrary—I was then in perfect health, enjoying a well-balanced mind and an *absolutely* tranquil spirit. Kitty and I entered Hamilton's shop together, and there, regardless of the order of affairs, I measured Kitty for the ring in the presence of the amused assistant. The ring was a sapphire with two diamonds. We men rode out down the slope that leads to the Combermere Bridge and Peliti's shop.

While my Waler was cautiously feeling his way over the loose shale, and Kitty was laughing and chattering at my side while all Simla, that is to say as much of it as had then come from the plains, was grouped round the reading-room and Peliti's verandah, I was aware that someone, apparently at a vast distance, was calling me by my Christian name. It struck me that I had heard the voice before, but when and where I could not at once determine. In the short space it took to cover the road between the path from Hamilton's shop and the first plank of the Combermere Bridge, I had thought over half a dozen people who might have committed such a solecism, and had eventually decided that it must have been some singing in my ears. Immediately opposite Peliti's shop my eye was arrested by the sight of four jhampanies in 'magpie' livery, pulling a yellow-panelled, cheap, bazaar 'rickshaw. In a moment my mind flew back to the previous season and Mrs Wessington, with a sense of irritation and disgust. Was it not enough that the woman was dead and done with, without her black and white servitors reappearing to spoil the day's happiness? Whoever employed them now, I thought I would call upon, and ask as a personal favour to change her jhampanies' livery. I would hire the men myself, and, if necessary, buy their coats from off their backs. It is impossible to say here what a flood of undesirable memories their presence evoked.

'Kitty,' I cried, 'there are poor Mrs Wessington's jhampanies turned up again! I wonder who has them now?'

Kitty had known Mrs Wessington slightly last season, and had always been interested in the sickly woman.

'What? Where?' she asked. 'I can't see them anywhere.'

Even as she spoke, her horse, swerving from a laden mule, threw himself directly in front of the advancing 'rickshaw. I had scarcely time to utter a word of warning when, to my unutterable horror, horse and rider passed *through* men and carriage as if they had been thin air.

'What's the matter?' cried Kitty; 'what made you call out so foolishly, Jack? If I *am* engaged I don't want all creation to know about it. There was lots of space between the mule and the verandah; and, if you think I can't ride—There!'

Whereupon the wilful Kitty set off, her dainty little head in the air, at a hand-gallop in the direction of the Bandstand; fully expecting, as she herself afterwards told me, that I should follow her. What was the matter? Nothing indeed. Either that I was mad or drunk, or that Simla was haunted with devils. I reined in my impatient cob, and turned round. The 'rickshaw had turned too, and now stood immediately facing me, near the left railing of the Combermere Bridge.

'Jack! Jack, darling!' (There was no mistake about the words this time: they rang through my brain as if they had been shouted in my ear.) 'It's some hideous mistake, I'm sure. *Please* forgive me, Jack, and let's be friends again.'

The 'rickshaw-hood had fallen back, and inside, as I hope and pray daily for the death I dread by night, sat Mrs Keith-Wessington, handkerchief in hand, and golden head bowed on her breast.

How long I stared motionless I do not know. Finally, I was aroused by my syce taking the Waler's bridle and asking whether I was ill. From the horrible to the commonplace is but a step. I tumbled off my horse and dashed, half-fainting, into Peliti's for a glass of cherry-brandy. There, two or three couples were gathered round the coffee-tables discussing the gossip of the day. Their trivialities were more comforting to me just then than the consolations of religion could have been. I plunged into the midst of the conversation at once; chatted, laughed and jested with a face (when I caught a glimpse of it in a mirror) as white and drawn as that of a corpse. Three or four men noticed my condition; and, evidently setting it down to the results of over-many pegs, charitably endeavoured to draw me apart from the rest of the loungers. But I refused to be led away. I wanted the company of my kind—as a child rushes into the midst of the dinner-party after a fright in the dark. I must have talked for about ten minutes or so, though it seemed an eternity to me, when I heard Kitty's clear voice outside enquiring for me. In another minute she had entered the shop, prepared to upbraid me for failing so signally in my duties. Something in my face stopped her.

'Why, Jack,' she cried, 'what *have* you been doing? What *has* happened? Are you ill?' Thus driven into a direct lie, I said that the sun had been a little too much for me. It was close upon five o'clock of a cloudy April afternoon, and the sun had been hidden all day. I saw my mistake as soon as the words were out of my mouth: attempted to recover it; blundered hopelessly and followed Kitty, in a regal rage, out of doors, amid the smiles of my acquaintances. I made some excuse (I have forgotten what) on the score of my feeling faint; and cantered away to my hotel, leaving Kitty to finish the ride by herself.

In my room I sat down and tried calmly to reason out the matter. Here was I, Theobald Jack Pansay, a well-educated Bengal Civilian in the year of grace, 1885, presumably sane, certainly healthy, driven in terror from my sweetheart's side by the apparition of a woman who had been dead and buried eight months ago. These were facts that I could not blink. Nothing was further from my thought than any memory of Mrs Wessington when Kitty and I left Hamilton's shop. Nothing was more utterly commonplace than the stretch of wall opposite Peliti's. It was broad daylight. The road was full of people; and yet here, look you, in defiance of every law of probability, in direct outrage of Nature's ordinance, there had appeared to me a face from the grave.

Kitty's Arab had gone *through* the 'rickshaw: so that my first hope that some woman marvellously like Mrs Wessington had hired the carriage and the coolies with their old livery was lost. Again and again I went round this treadmill of thought; and again and again gave up baffled and in despair. The voice was as inexplicable as the apparition. I had originally some wild notion of confiding it all to Kitty; of begging her to marry me at once; and in her arms defying the ghostly occupant of the 'rickshaw. 'After all,' I argued, 'the presence of the 'rickshaw is in itself enough to prove the existence of a spectral illusion. One may see ghosts of men and women, but surely never coolies and carriages. The whole thing is absurd. Fancy the ghost of a hillman!'

Next morning I sent a penitent note to Kitty, imploring her to overlook my strange conduct of the previous afternoon. My Divinity was still very wroth, and a personal apology was necessary. I explained, with a fluency born of night-long pondering over a falsehood, that I had been attacked with a sudden palpitation of the heart—the result of indigestion. This eminently practical solution had its effect: and Kitty and I rode out that afternoon with the shadow of my first lie dividing us.

Nothing would please her save a canter round Jakko. With my nerves still unstrung from the previous night I feebly protested against the notion, suggesting Observatory Hill, Jutogh, the Boileaugunge road—anything rather than the Jakko round. Kitty was angry and a little hurt; so I yielded from fear of provoking further misunderstanding, and we set out together towards Chhota Simla. We walked a greater part of the way, and, according to our custom, cantered from a mile or so below the Convent to the stretch of level road by the Sanjowlie Reservoir. The wretched horses appeared to fly, and my heart beat quicker and quicker as we neared the crest of the ascent. My mind had been full of Mrs Wessington all afternoon; and every inch of the Jakko road bore witness to our old-time walks and talks. The bowlders were full of it; the pines sang it aloud overhead; the rain-fed torrents giggled and chuckled unseen over the shameful story; and the wind in my ears chanted the iniquity aloud.

As a fitting climax, in the middle of the level men call the Ladies' Mile, the horror was awaiting me. No other 'rickshaw was in sight—only the four black and white jhampanies, the yellow-panelled carriage, and the golden head of the woman within—all apparently just as I had left them eight months and one fortnight ago! For an instant I fancied that Kitty *must* see what I saw—we were so marvellously sympathetic in all things.

Her next words undeceived me—'Not a soul in sight! Come along, Jack, and I'll race you to the Reservoir buildings!' Her wiry little Arab was off like a bird, my Waler following close behind, and in this order we dashed under the cliffs. Half a minute brought us within fifty yards of the 'rickshaw. I pulled my Waler and fell back a little. The 'rickshaw was directly in the middle of the road; and once more the Arab passed through it, my horse following. 'Jack! Jack dear! *Please* forgive me,' rang with a wail in my ears, and, after an interval: 'It's all a mistake, a hideous mistake!'

I spurred my horse like a man possessed. When I turned my head at the Reservoir works, the black and white liveries were still waiting—patiently waiting—under the grey hillside, and the wind brought me a mocking echo of the words I had just heard. Kitty bantered me a good deal on my silence throughout the remainder of the ride. I had been talking, up till then, wildly and at random. To save my life I could not speak afterwards, naturally, and from Sanjowlie to the Church wisely held my tongue.

I was to dine with the Mannerings that night, and had barely time to canter home to dress. On the road to Elysium Hill I overheard two men talking together in the dusk—'It's a curious thing,' said one, 'how completely all trace of it disappeared. You know my wife was insanely fond of the woman (never could see anything in her myself), and wanted me to pick up her old 'rickshaw and coolies if they were to be got for love or money. Morbid sort of fancy I call it; but I've got to do what the Memsahib tells me. Would you believe that the man she hired it from tells me that all four of the men—they were brothers—died of cholera on the way to Haridwar, poor devils; and the 'rickshaw has been broken up by the man himself. Told me he never used a dead Memsahib's 'rickshaw. Spoilt his luck. Queer notion, wasn't it? Fancy poor little Mrs Wessington spoiling anyone's luck except her own!' I laughed aloud at this point; and my laugh jarred on me as I uttered it. So there *were* ghosts of 'rickshaws after all, and ghostly employments in the other world! How much did Mrs Wessington give her men? What were their hours? Where did they go?

And for visible answer to my last question I saw the infernal thing blocking my path in the twilight. The dead travel fast, and by short cuts unknown to ordinary coolies. I laughed aloud a second time and checked my laughter suddenly, for I was afraid I was going mad. Mad to a certain extent I must have been, for I recollect that I reined in my horse at the head of the 'rickshaw, and politely wished Mrs Wessington 'Good-evening'. Her answer was one I knew only too well. I listened to the end; and replied that I had heard it all before, but should be delighted if she had anything further to say; some malignant devil stronger than I must have entered into me that evening, for I have a dim recollection of talking the commonplaces of the day for five minutes to the thing in front of me.

'Mad as a hatter, poor devil—or drunk. Max, try and get him to come home.'

Surely *that* was not Mrs Wessington's voice! The two men had overheard me speaking to the empty air, and had returned to look after me. They were very kind and considerate, and from their words evidently gathered that I was extremely drunk. I thanked them confusedly and cantered away to my hotel; there changed, and arrived at the Mannerings' ten minutes late. I pleaded the darkness of the night as an excuse; was rebuked by Kitty for my unlover-like tardiness; and sat down.

The conversation had already become general; and under cover of it, I was addressing some tender small talk to my sweetheart when I was aware that at the further end of the table a short red-whiskered man was describing, with much broidery, his encounter with a mad unknown that evening.

A few sentences convinced me that he was repeating the incident of half an hour ago. In the middle of the story he looked around for applause, as professional storytellers do, caught my eye, and straightway collapsed. There was a moment's awkward silence, and the red-whiskered man muttered something to the effect that he had 'forgotten the rest', thereby sacrificing a reputation as a good storyteller which he had built up for six seasons past. I blessed him from the bottom of my heart, and—went on with my fish.

In the fullness of time, that dinner came to an end; and with genuine regret I tore myself away from Kitty—as certain as I was of my own existence that it would be waiting for me outside the door. The red-whiskered man, who had been introduced to me as Dr Heatherlegh of Simla, volunteered to bear me company as far as our roads lay together. I accepted his offer with gratitude.

My instinct had not deceived me. It lay in readiness in the Mall, and, in what seemed devilish mockery of our ways, with a lighted head lamp. The red-whiskered man went to the point at once, in a manner that showed he had been thinking over it all dinner-time.

'I say, Pansay, what the deuce was the matter with you this evening on the Elysium Road?' The suddenness of the question wrenched an answer from me before I was aware.

'That!' said I, pointing to it.

'*That* may be either D.T. or eyes for aught I know. Now you don't liquor. I saw as much at dinner, so it can't be D.T. There's nothing whatever where you're pointing, though you're sweating and trembling with fright, like a scared pony. Therefore, I conclude that it's eyes. And I ought to understand all about them Come along home with me. I'm on the Blessington lower road.'

To my intense delight, the 'rickshaw, instead of waiting for us, kept about twenty yards ahead—and this, too, whether we walked, trotted, or cantered. In the course of that long night ride I had told my companion almost as much as I have told you here.

'Well, you've spoilt one of the best tales I've ever laid tongue to,' said he, 'but I'll forgive you for the sake of what you've gone through. Now come home and do what I tell you; and when I've cured you, young man, let this be a lesson to you to steer clear of women and indigestible food till the day of your death.'

The 'rickshaw kept steady in front; and my red-whiskered friend seemed to derive great pleasure from my account of its exact whereabouts.

'Eyes, Pansay—all eyes, brain and stomach. And the greatest of these three is stomach. You've too much conceited brain, too little stomach, and thoroughly unhealthy eyes. Get your stomach straight and the rest follows. And all that's French for a liver pill. I'll take sole medical charge of you from this hour! For you're too interesting a phenomenon to be passed over.'

By this time we were deep in the shadow of the Blessington lower road and the 'rickshaw came to a dead stop under a pine-clad, overhanging shale cliff. Instinctively I halted too, giving my reason, Heatherlegh rapped out an oath.

'Now, if you think I'm going to spend a cold night on the hillside for the sake of a stomach-cum-brain-cum-eye illusion— Lord have mercy! What's that?'

There was a muffled report, a blinding smother of dust just in front of us, a crack, the noise of rent boughs, and about ten yards of the cliff-side—pines, undergrowth, and all—slid down into the road below, completely blocking it up. The uprooted trees swayed and tottered for a moment like drunken giants in the gloom, and then fell prone among their fellows with a thunderous crash. Our two horses stood motionless and sweating with fear. As soon as the rattle of falling earth and stone had subsided, my companion muttered: 'Man, if we'd gone forward we should have been ten-feet deep in our graves by now. "There are more things in heaven and earth…" Come home, Pansay, and thank God. I want a peg badly.'

We retraced our way over the Church Ridge, and I arrived at Dr Heatherlegh's house shortly after midnight.

His attempts towards my cure commenced almost immediately, and for a week I never left his sight. Many a time in the course of that week did I bless the good fortune which had thrown me in contact with Simla's best and kindest doctor. Day by day my spirits grew lighter and more equable. Day by day, too, I became more and more inclined to fall in with Heatherlegh's 'spectral illusion' theory, implicating the eyes, brain, and stomach. I wrote to Kitty, telling her that a slight sprain caused by a fall from my horse kept me indoors for a few days; and that I should be recovered before she had time to regret my absence.

Heatherlegh's treatment was simple to a degree. It consisted of liver pills, cold-water baths, and strong exercise, taken in the dusk or at early dawn—for, as he sagely observed: 'A man with a sprained ankle doesn't walk a dozen miles a day, and your young woman might be wondering if she saw you.'

At the end of the week, after much examination of pupil and pulse, and strict injunctions as to diet and pedestrianism, Heatherlegh dismissed me as brusquely as he had taken charge of me. Here is his parting benediction: 'Man, I certify to your mental cure, and that's as much as to say I've cured most of your bodily ailments. Now, get your traps out of this as soon as you can; and be off to make love to Miss Kitty.'

I was endeavouring to express my thanks for his kindness. He cut me short.

'Don't think I did this because I like you. I gather that you've behaved like a blackguard all through. But, all the same, you're a phenomenon, and as queer a phenomenon as you are a blackguard. No!'—checking me a second time—'not a rupee, please. Go out and see if you can find the eyes-brain-and-stomach business again. I'll give you a lakh for each time you see it.'

Half an hour later I was in the Mannerings' drawing-room with Kitty—drunk with the intoxication of the present happiness and the foreknowledge that I should never more be troubled with its hideous presence. Strong in the sense of my new-found security, I proposed a ride at once; and, by preference, a canter round Jakko.

Never had I felt so well, so overladen with vitality and mere animal spirits, as I did on the afternoon of the 30 April. Kitty was delighted at the change in my appearance, and complimented me on it in her delightfully frank and outspoken manner. We left the Mannerings' house together, laughing and talking, and cantered along the Chhota Simla road as of old.

I was in haste to reach the Sanjowlie Reservoir and there make my assurance doubly sure. The horses did their best, but seemed all too slow to my impatient mind. Kitty was astonished at my boisterousness. 'Why, Jack!' she cried at last, 'you are behaving like a child. What are you doing?'

We were just below the Convent, and from sheer wantonness I was making my Waler plunge and curvet across the road as I tickled it with the loop of my riding-whip.

'Doing?' I answered; 'nothing, dear. That's just it. If you'd been doing nothing for a week except lie up, you'd be as riotous as I.

'Singing and murmuring in your feastful mirth,
Joying to feel yourself alive;
Lord over Nature, Lord of the visible Earth,
Lord of the senses five.'

My quotation was hardly out of my lips before we had rounded the corner above the Convent; and a few yards further on could see across to Sanjowlie. In the centre of the level road stood the black and white liveries, the yellow-panelled 'rickshaw, and Mrs Keith-Wessington. I pulled up, looked, rubbed my eyes, and, I believe, must have said something. The next thing I knew was that I was lying face downward on the road, with Kitty kneeling above me in tears.

'Has it gone, child?' I gasped. Kitty only wept more bitterly.

'Has what gone, Jack dear? What does it all mean? There must be a mistake somewhere, Jack. A hideous mistake.' Her last words brought me to my feet—mad—raving for the time being.

'Yes, there *is* a mistake somewhere,' I repeated, 'a hideous mistake. Come and look at It.'

I have an indistinct idea that I dragged Kitty by the wrist along the road up to where It stood, and implored her for pity's sake to speak to It; to tell It that we were betrothed; that neither Death nor Hell could break the tie between us: and Kitty only knows how much more to the same effect. Now and again I appealed passionately to the Terror in the 'rickshaw to bear witness to all I had said, and to release me from a torture that was killing me. As I talked I suppose I must have told Kitty of my old relations with Mrs Wessington, for I saw her listen intently with a white face and blazing eyes.

'Thank you, Mr Pansay,' she said, 'that's *quite* enough. Syce, *ghora lao.*'

The syces, impassive as Orientals always are, had come up

with the recaptured horses; and as Kitty sprang into her saddle I caught hold of her bridle, entreating her to hear me out and forgive. My answer was the cut of her riding-whip across my face from mouth to eye, and a word or two of farewell that even now I cannot write down. So I judged and judged rightly, that Kitty knew all; and I staggered back to the side of the 'rickshaw. My face was cut and bleeding, and the blow of the riding-whip had raised a livid blue wheal on it. I had no self-respect. Just then, Heatherlegh, who must have been following Kitty and me at a distance, cantered up.

'Doctor,' I said, pointing to my face, 'here's Miss Mannering's signature to my order of dismissal and I'll thank you for that lakh as soon as convenient.'

Heatherlegh's face, even in my abject miser, moved me to laughter.

'I'll stake my professional reputation,' he began.

'Don't be a fool,' I whispered. 'I've lost my life's happiness and you'd better take me home.'

As I spoke the 'rickshaw was gone. Then I lost all knowledge of what was passing. The crest of Jakko seemed to heave and roll like the crest of a cloud and fall in upon me.

Seven days later (on 7 May, that is to say) I was aware that I was lying in Heatherlegh's room as weak as a little child. Heatherlegh was watching me intently from behind the papers on his writing-table. His first words were not encouraging; but I was too far spent to be much moved by them.

'Here's Miss Kitty has sent back your letters. You corresponded a good deal, you young people. Here's a packet that looks like a ring and a cheerful sort of a note from Mannering Papa, which I've taken the liberty of reading and burning. The old gentleman's not pleased with you.'

'And Kitty?' I asked dully.

'Rather more drawn than her father from what she says. By the same token you must have been letting out any number of queer reminiscences just before I met you. Says that a man who would have behaved to a woman as you did to Mrs Wessington ought to kill himself out of sheer pity for his kind. She's a hot-headed little virago, your mash. Will have it too that you were suffering from D.T. when that row on the Jakko road turned up. Says she'll die before she ever speaks to you again.'

I groaned and turned over on the other side.

'Now you've got your choice, my friend. This engagement has to be broken off; and the Mannerings don't want to be too hard on you. Was it broken through D.T. or epileptic fits? Sorry I can't offer you a better exchange unless you'd prefer hereditary insanity. Say the word and I'll tell 'em it's fits. All Simla knows about that scene on the Ladies' Mile. Come! I'll give you five minutes to think over it.'

During those five minutes I believe that I explored thoroughly the lowest circles of the inferno which man is permitted to tread on earth. And at the same time I was watching myself faltering through the dark labyrinths of doubt, misery and utter despair. I wondered, as Heatherlegh in his chair might have wondered, which dreadful alternative I should adopt. Presently I heard myself answering in a voice that I hardly recognized—

'They're confoundedly particular about morality in these parts. Give 'em fits, Heatherlegh, and my love. Now let me sleep a bit longer.'

Then my two selves joined, and it was only I (half-crazed, devil-driven I) that tossed in my bed tracing step by step the history of the past month.

'But I am in Simla,' I kept repeating to myself. 'I, Jack Pansay am in Simla, and there are no ghosts here. It's unreasonable of that woman to pretend there are. Why couldn't Agnes have left me alone? I never did her any harm. It might just as well have been me as Agnes. Only I'd never have come back on purpose to kill *her*. Why can't I be left alone—left alone and happy?'

It was high noon when I first awoke: and the sun was low in the sky before I slept—slept as the tortured criminal sleeps on his rack, too worn to feel further pain.

Next day I could not leave my bed. Heatherlegh told me in the morning that he had received an answer from Mr Mannering, and that, thanks to his (Heatherlegh's) friendly offices, the story of my affliction had travelled through the length and breadth of Simla, where I was on all sides much pitied.

'And that's rather more than you deserve,' he concluded pleasantly, 'though the Lord knows you've been going through a pretty severe mill. Never mind; we'll cure you yet, you perverse phenomenon.'

I declined firmly to be cured. 'You've been much too good to me already, old man,' said I; 'but I don't think I need trouble you further.'

In my heart I knew that nothing Heatherlegh could do would lighten the burden that had been laid upon me.

With that knowledge came also a sense of hopeless, impotent rebellion against the unreasonableness of it all. There were scores of men no better than I whose punishments had at least been reserved for another world; and I felt that it was bitterly, cruelly unfair that I alone should have been singled out for so hideous a fate. This mood would in time give place to another where it seemed that the 'rickshaw and I were the only realities in a world of shadows; that Kitty was a ghost; that Mannering, Heatherlegh, and all the other men and women I knew were all ghosts; and the great, grey hills themselves but vain shadows devised to torture me. From mood to mood I tossed backwards and forwards for seven weary days; my body growing daily stronger and stronger, until the bedroom looking-glass told me that I had returned to everyday life, and was as other men once more. Curiously enough my face showed no signs of the struggle I had gone through. It was pale indeed, but as expressionless and commonplace as ever. I had expected some permanent alteration—visible evidence of the disease that was eating me away. I found nothing.

On 15 May, I left Heatherlegh's house at eleven o'clock in the morning; and the instinct of the bachelor drove me to the club. There I found that every man knew my story as told by Heatherlegh, and was, in clumsy fashion, abnormally kind and attentive. Nevertheless, I recognized that for the rest of my natural life I should be among but not of my fellows; and I envied very bitterly indeed the laughing coolies on the Mall below. I lunched at the club, and at four o'clock wandered aimlessly down the Mall in the vague hope of meeting Kitty. Close to the Bandstand the black and white liveries joined me; and I heard Mrs Wessington's old appeal at my side. I had been expecting this ever since I came out; and was only surprised at her delay. The phantom 'rickshaw and I went side by side along the Chhota Simla road in silence. Close to the bazar, Kitty and a man on horseback overtook and passed us. For any sign she gave I might have been a dog on the road. She did not even pay me the compliment of quickening her pace; though the rainy afternoon had served for an excuse.

So Kitty and her companion, and I and my ghostly Light-o'-Love, crept round Jakko in couples. The road was streaming with water; the pines dripped like roof-pipes on the rocks below, and the air was full of fine, driving rain. Two or three times I found myself saying to myself almost aloud: 'I'm Jack Pansay on leave at Simla—*at Simla!* Everyday, ordinary Simla. I mustn't forget that—I mustn't forget that.' Then I would try to recollect some of the gossip I had heard at the Club: the prices of so-and-so's horses—anything, in fact, that related to the work-a-day Anglo-Indian world I knew so well. I even repeated the multiplication table rapidly to myself, to make quite sure that I was not taking leave of my senses. It gave me much comfort; and must have prevented my hearing Mrs Wessington for a time.

Once more I wearily climbed the Convent slope and entered the level road. Here Kitty and the man started off at a canter, and I was left alone with Mrs Wessington. 'Agnes,' said I, 'will you put back your hood and tell me what it all means?' The hood dropped noiselessly, and I was face to face with my dead and buried mistress. She was wearing the dress in which I had last seen her alive; carried the same tiny handkerchief in her right hand; and the same card-case in her left. (A woman eight months dead with a card-case!) I had to pin myself down to the multiplication table, and to set both hands on the stone parapet of the road, to assure myself that that at least was real.

'Agnes,' I repeated, 'for pity's sake tell me what it all means.' Mrs Wessington leaned forward, with that odd, quick turn of the head I used to know so well, and spoke.

If my story had not already so madly overleaped the bounds of all human belief I should apologize to you now. As I know that no one—no, not even Kitty, for whom it is written as some sort of justification of my conduct—will believe me, I will go on. Mrs Wessington spoke and I walked with her from the Sanjowlie road to the turning below the Commander-in-Chief's house as I might walk by the side of any living woman's 'rickshaw, deep in conversation. The second and most tormenting of my moods of sickness had suddenly laid hold upon me, and like the prince in Tennyson's poem, 'I seemed to move amid a world of ghosts.' There had been a garden-party at the Commander-in-Chief's, and we two joined the crowd of homeward-bound folk. As I saw them, it seemed that *they* were the shadows—impalpable fantastic shadows—that divided for Mrs Wessington's 'rickshaw to pass through. What we said during the course of that weird interview I cannot—indeed, I dare not—tell. Heatherlegh's comment would have been a short laugh and a remark that I had been 'mashing a brain-eye-and-stomach chimera'. It was a ghastly and, yet in some indefinable way, a marvellously dear experience. Could it be possible, I wondered, that I was in this life to woo a second time the woman I had killed by my own neglect and cruelty?

I met Kitty on the homeward road—a shadow among shadows. If I were to describe all the incidents of the next fortnight in their order, my story would never come to an end; and your patience would be exhausted. Morning after morning and evening after evening the ghostly 'rickshaw and I used to wander through Simla together. Wherever I went the four black and white liveries followed me and bore me company to and from my hotel. At the theatre I found them amid the crowd of yelling jhampanies; outside the club verandah, after a long evening of whist; at the Birthday Ball, waiting patiently for my reappearance; and in broad daylight when I went calling. Save that it cast no shadow, the 'rickshaw was in every respect as real to look upon as one of wood and iron. More than once, indeed, I have had to check myself from warning some hard-riding friend against cantering over it. More than once I have walked down the Mall deep in conversation with Mrs Wessington to the unspeakable amazement of the passersby.

Before I had been out and about a week I learned that the 'fit' theory had been discarded in favour of insanity. However, I made no change in my mode of life. I called, rode, and dined out as freely as ever. I had a passion for the society of my kind which I had never felt before; I hungered to be among the realities of life; and at the same time I felt vaguely unhappy when I had been separated too long from my ghostly companion. It would be almost impossible to describe my varying moods from 15 May up to today.

The presence of the 'rickshaw filled me by turns with horror, blind fear, a dim sort of pleasure, and utter despair. I dared not leave Simla; and I knew that my stay there was killing me. I knew, moreover, that it was my destiny to die slowly and a little every day. My only anxiety was to get the penance over as quietly as might be. Alternately, I hungered for a sight of Kitty, and watched her outrageous flirtations with my successor—to speak more accurately, my successors—with amused interest. She was as much out of my life as I was out of hers. By day I wandered with Mrs Wessington almost content. By night I implored Heaven to let me return to the world as I used to know it. Above all these varying moods lay the sensation of dull, numbing wonder that the seen and the unseen should mingle so strangely on this earth to hound one poor soul to its grave.

August, 27—Heatherlegh has been indefatigable in his attendance on me; and only yesterday told me that I ought to send in an application for sick leave. An application to escape the company of a phantom! A request that the government would graciously permit me to get rid of five ghosts and an airy 'rickshaw by going to England! Heatherlegh's proposition moved me to almost hysterical laughter. I told him that I should await the end quietly at Simla; and I am sure that the end is not far off. Believe me that I dread its advent more than any word can say; and I torture myself nightly with a thousand speculations as to the manner of my death. Shall I die in my bed decently and as an English gentleman should die; or, in one last walk on the Mall, will my soul be wrenched from me to take its place forever and ever by the side of that ghastly phantasm? Shall I return to my old lost allegiance in the next world, or shall I meet Agnes loathing her and bound to her side through all eternity? Shall we two hover over the scene of our lives till the end of time? As the day of my death draws nearer, the intense horror that all living flesh feels toward escaped spirits from beyond the grave grows more and more powerful. It is an awful thing to go down quick among the dead with scarcely one-half of our life completed. It is a thousand times more awful to wait as I do in your midst, for I know not what unimaginable terror. Pity me, at least on the score of my 'delusion', for I know you will never believe what I have written here. Yet as surely as ever a man was done to death by the Powers of Darkness, I am that man. In justice, too, pity her. For as surely as ever a woman was killed by a man, I killed Mrs Wessington. And the last portion of my punishment is even now upon me.

THE WHITE TIGER

Alice Perrin

He was called the White Tiger by the villagers of the district because his yellow skin was pale with age, and his stripes so faded and far apart as to be almost invisible.

Having grown too large and heavy for cattle-killing with any ease, he had lately become a man-eater, and terrible were the stories told by those who had seen him and escaped the fatal blow of his huge paw. He was described as being the size of a bull-buffalo, with a belly that reached the ground, and a white moon between his ears, true tokens of the man-eater, as every native of India knows. He was said to have the power of assuming different shapes, and to lure his prey by the imitation of a human voice, and certainly his craft and cunning were such that not even Mar Singh, the local shikaree, had ever been able to trap him, or obtain a shot at him with his famous match-lock gun. And, Mar Singh had seen the tiger often, knew his favourite haunts and lairs, and could point out the very trees upon which he preferred to sharpen his murderous claws.

The brute continued to levy his terrible tax on the scanty population of a remote district, until the women and children were afraid to leave the village, and the men went out to work in the fields fearing for their lives.

At last, the increasing number of victims attracted the attention of the local authorities, and a reward of a hundred rupees was placed on the head of the White Tiger, with the result that Mar Singh, who clothed himself in khaki with a disreputable turban to match, and was regarded in his village as the wariest of hunters, redoubled his efforts to bring about the destruction of this awful scourge. Also, now that the fame of the White Tiger's misdeeds had penetrated to the headquarters, it was more than likely that a party of 'sahibs' would appear on the scene with elephants and rifles, in which case, though the tiger would be doomed, the reward would be distributed amongst the mahouts and the heaters, and Mar Singh himself would only receive a share.

So, night after night he perched on the branches of the trees above the favourite routes of the enemy, and from sunrise to sunset he haunted the outskirts of the jungle, and hung about the drinking-pools in the bed of the shrinking river, for (unlike his cattle and game-killing brothers) the man-eater may be sought for at all hours. But to no purpose, the White Tiger seized a plump human victim once every few days, and Mar Singh's vision of the reward grew faint.

'The striped one is surely an evil spirit, and no beast at all!' said Mar Singh, who never uttered the word tiger if he could help it, for fear of ill-luck.

He had come in weary and crestfallen from a long day's search, having actually caught a glimpse of the White Tiger, and followed the tracks of the huge, square pugs to the edge of a thorny thicket, without the chance of a shot that could have taken effect; and he was pouring out his irritation and disgust to Kowta, his half-brother, who sat at the door of the family hovel contentedly smoking a hookah.

'Without doubt,' agreed Kowta, 'and therefore, would it not be wiser to let the sahib slay the Evil One if he be able?'

'What sahib?' asked Mar Singh sharply, pausing in the act of cleaning the precious match-lock gun, which was the envy and admiration of the village.

'Then thou has not heard the news?' said Kowta, innocently. 'A sahib has pitched his camp within one day's march of the village, and they say he has come to hunt the White Devil.'

The dreaded blow had fallen, and Mar Singh danced with rage.

'I will give him no news of the tiger. I will tell him nothing, and see, too, that thou remainest silent, Kowta, when he sends for information, else it will be the worse for thee!'

Kowta twiddled his big toe in the dust, always a sign of hesitation with a native, and Mar Singh scented trouble. He knew that Kowta was heavily in debt to the village usurer, and that sahibs often paid well for news of a tiger's movements. He was also aware that Kowta was jealous of his standing and reputation in the village, which would be increased ten-fold could he but destroy the tiger and earn the magnificent reward.

He changed his tone.

'See, brother,' he began insinuatingly, 'the utmost that the sahib would give thee might, perchance, be ten rupees, and thy share of the Government reward would scarcely be more than two. What are twelve rupees compared with forty, added to half the whiskers and claws of the Evil One, and perhaps, the lucky bone as well? All this will I give thee when I slay the beast, as I most assuredly must do if the sahib doth not interfere.'

Kowta puffed stolidly at his hookah and was maddeningly silent.

'Also,' continued Mar Singh, eagerly, 'consider the trouble that a sahib's camp brings upon a village. His servants, being rascals, will order supplies in the name of the sahib, and pay us nothing for them, and the police will annoy us if we complain. We shall be forced to beat the jungle, and many will be hurt and some killed, if not by the tiger then by other wild beasts, also?—'

'But how am I to tell that thou wilt give me the forty rupees and half the claws and whiskers? Whereas, a sahib holds to his promises, as we all know.'

'I swear it!' cried Mar Singh with fervour, 'by the skin of the White Devil I swear to deal well by thee!'

So, after some further argument, Kowta reluctantly agreed to take his brother's side, and Mar Singh unfolded a scheme by which Kowta was to proceed to the tents of the unwelcome Englishman, and pose as the shikaree of the district, possessing an intimate knowledge of the tiger's habits. Mar Singh would keep Kowta well-informed as to the movements of the tiger through the medium of the postman who ran from village to village with news and letters, and the sahib, at all hazards, was to be led in the wrong directions, until he grew weary of the fruitless chase, and withdrew from the district with his camp and elephants.

Kowta, therefore, proceeded to don the khaki costume, which he had long coveted, and the next morning he started on his diplomatic errand, while Mar Singh betook himself to the jungle to watch the movements of the White Tiger, that he might warn Kowta by the evening runner as to which locality must be avoided the following day.

Kowta enjoyed himself immensely at the camp. He arrived at sundown, and was interviewed by the sahib himself, to whom he gave voluble, but entirely false, information concerning the tiger, and promised to lead him direct to the animal's lair in the morning. The sahib, being young and new to the country, retired to bed in happy anticipation, and Kowta repaired to the kitchen tent, where, surrounded by the servants, he sat smoking his hookah and relating blood-curdling tales of the doings of the White Tiger.

Natives seldom sleep till far on in the night, and therefore, the gathering was at its height when the jingle of bells told of the postman's approach, and Kowta, explaining to the company that he was expecting news of his dying grandmother, went out into the moonlight to meet him. The chink-chink of the bunch of bells grew louder, and mingled with the regular grunts of the runner, and Kowta, stepping-forward into the sandy path, checked the man's rapid trot.

'Oh, brother!' he saluted, 'what word from Mar Singh, shikaree?'

'Kowta, there is no word from the mouth of Mar Singh, thy brother, seeing that but an hour after thy departure he was slain by the White Tiger on the outskirts of the grazing plain, and Merijhan, the cow-herd, saw it happen. I bring the evil news to thee, fresh from thy village.'

For a moment Kowta was paralysed by the horror of the dreadful and unexpected news. Then he asked questions, and learned that his brother's body had been recovered by a party of villagers who had sallied forth with drums and fireworks and had driven the beast from its prey. The mangled remains now lay in the family hut, and Kowta's presence was required to make arrangements for the funeral.

Kowta slipped some coppers into the postman's willing hand, and charged him to keep silence as to the catastrophe when delivering letters in the camp. Then he collected his belongings, and left a plausible message for the sahib to say he had been summoned to his grandmother's deathbed, but would return with all haste the following day. He set out in the moonlight along the narrow jungle path, bordered by tall grass higher than his head, and walked rapidly, though the heat was overpowering, until, just as the dawn broke, he came within sight of the village. He strode through the fields of tobacco and young wheat, and saw the bright green parrots flashing to and fro in the vivid yellow light; partridges ran from beneath his feet, calling shrilly as they disappeared behind the clumps of dry grass; and he could hear the jungle fowl in the distance crowing to the rising sun. Everything was awake and glowing with life, and the dark interior of the hut, where the women were wailing and the atmosphere seemed charged with death, formed a sharp contrast to the outside world.

The mangled body of the dead man, torn and chewed by the tiger, lay on the string bedstead, surrounded by a noisy group of mourning relatives. There was nothing for Kowta to do but arrange for the remains to be taken to the burning-ground in the evening and to attempt to pacify the wailing throng, until, as the fierce, hot noon came on, they gradually dispersed, and even the widow of the dead man sought a siesta in a neighbour's hut, while Kowta sat down on the threshold of his home to think.

An idea had been slowly forming in his brain which brought with it a wave of exultation. Why should not he compass the destruction of the White Tiger, and so earn the whole reward. He was in debt to the moneylender, and he also greatly desired a plot of land that was for sale just outside the village, and the hundred rupees would not only free him from debt, but would also purchase the coveted little piece of ground. It was true that Mar Singh himself had never succeeded in shooting the White Tiger, but then his difficulty had always been the want of suitable bait, whereas *now*—Kowta glanced back into the shadow of the hut and shivered, remembering the native belief that the soul of the tiger's victim becomes the servant of the slayer, and is bound to warn the master when danger threatens.

Mar Singh's spirit might or might not be in bondage to the White Tiger, but, in any case, the hundred rupees was worth some risk, and with proper precautions there should be little or no danger, seeing that the match-lock gun had been recovered uninjured. Kowta rose and looked up and down the little village street. Not a breeze stirred the giant leaves of the plantain trees, not a bird uttered a note, not a voice broke the breathless calm; every creature except himself was wrapped in slumber.

He made up his mind. He would attempt the plan, and afterwards, whether he succeeded or failed, he could deny all knowledge of the disappearance of his brother's body, and encourage the suggestion which would naturally arise, that the sorcery of the White Tiger had spirited the corpse away. So, he gathered the wreck of Mar Singh into a bundle, wrapping it in his own white cotton-waste waist-cloth, and with the loaded match-lock over his shoulder, went swiftly through the sleeping village and out into the fields, invoking on his errand the blessing of Durga, the goddess who rides the tiger. Thence, he took a narrow jungle path with tangled shrubs closing over his head, and as he emerged from this on to the bushy, broken ground leading to the river, he gathered a leaf from the nearest tree and muttered—

'As thy life has departed, so may the striped one die.'

He walked up the pebbly bed of the dwindling stream till he reached a pool of clear water, in the wet margin of which were printed countless tracks of animals that had drunk there during the night. Wild pig, jackal, fox, hyena, all had satiated their thirst, but the White Tiger had not been of the company. A hundred yards off lay another pool, and around it Kowta found a solitary track—the big, square pugs of the beast who, by common consent of the other jungle inhabitants, had been given a wide berth, and allowed to drink alone.

The marks were not more than a few hours old, and Kowta followed them cautiously, grasping the gun and dragging his other burden behind him along the gravelly sand. The footprints led him to some rocky boulders, on the summit of which a family of monkeys sat peacefully hunting for fleas, a sign that the tiger was not on the move, else they would have been crashing and chattering in the nearest trees, and pouring forth torrents of abuse. The pugs led on round the rocks to a shady thicket of thorn bushes in a deep ravine, and Kowta felt that he had tracked the White Tiger to his lair.

He laid his brother's body close to the edge of the thorny thicket, and then cast about for a safe retreat within easy shot, but no climbable trees were at hand, the cover consisting of low, scrubby bushes. The only suitable place of concealment seemed to be the nearest rock, behind which it would be easy to hide and yet command a good view of the bait.

The odour of the dead body tainted the air as the sun blazed full upon it, which suited Kowta's purpose well, for tigers prefer their food as carrion, and hunger would soon bring the beast forth. Kowta lay down behind the rock and waited. A hot, high wind was blowing, and the sand from the riverbed, getting into his eyes, made them smart, but he paid no heed to the discomfort, and only watched the thicket intently for the least movement.

He held his breath when, presently, something rustled and crept out—merely a mangy little jackal with loosely-hanging brush, who sprang four feet into the air as he came suddenly on Mar Singh's body. Then the animal uttered the long, miserable wail known as the 'pheeaow cry,' and ran back into the thicket, causing Kowta's heart to beat high with hope, for he knew the jackal was a 'provider', one that gives notice to the tiger when food is to be found.

Now, without doubt the Evil One would steal forth, and nothing could then prevent a shot at such close quarters taking effect. A pea-fowl screeched wildly, and Kowta could hear the agitated flapping of its wings, that also was a token that the tiger moved. The monkeys set up a clatter and scuttled from the rocks. He was coming—the White Devil, the evil striped one!

Kowta waited breathless, his pulses throbbing in his ears, thinking of the hundred rupees and the plot of ground that were now almost his own, and gazing fixedly over the sickening, twisted limbs of the mutilated body only a few yards from him.

The tension was terrible, and the cracking of a dry twig behind him sounded almost like the report of a gun, he felt a surging in his brain, and, as another stick snapped, some irresistible power compelled him to turn his head.

There, five yards behind him, crouched the White Tiger, that with silent steps and awful cunning had stalked him from the village. The ears were flattened to the broad head, the long white whiskers bristled and quivered, the wicked yellow eyes glared, and held the man helpless, spellbound with horror, waiting for the spring that came with a hissing, growling roar, as the White Tiger claimed yet another victim.

THE INTERLOPERS

'Saki' (H.H. Munro)

In a forest of mixed growth somewhere on the eastern spurs of the Carpathians, a man stood one winter night watching and listening, as though he waited for some beast of the woods to come within the range of his vision, and, later, of his rifle. But the game for whose presence he kept so keen an outlook was none that figured in the sportsman's calendar as lawful and proper for the chase; Ulrich von Gradwitz patrolled the dark forest in quest of a human enemy.

The forest lands of Gradwitz were of wide extent and well stocked with game; the narrow strip of precipitous woodland that lay on its outskirt was not remarkable for the game it harboured or the shooting it afforded, but it was the most jealously guarded of all its owner's territorial possessions. A famous lawsuit, in the days of his grandfather, had wrested it from the illegal possession of a neighbouring family of petty landowners; the dispossessed party had never acquiesced in the judgment of the Courts, and a long series of poaching affrays and similar scandals had embittered the relationships between the families for three generations. The neighbour feud had grown into a personal one since Ulrich had come to be head of his family; if there was a man in the world whom he detested and wished ill to it was George Znaeym, the inheritor of the quarrel and the tireless game-snatcher and raider of the disputed border-forest. The feud might, perhaps, have died down or been compromised if the personal ill-will of the two men had not stood in the way; as boys they had thirsted for one another's blood, as men each prayed that misfortune might fall on the other, and this wind-scourged winter night Ulrich had banded together his foresters to watch the dark forest, not in quest of four-footed quarry, but to keep a long-out for the prowling thieves whom he suspected of being afoot from across the land boundary. The roebuck, which usually kept in the sheltered hollows during a storm-wind, were running like driven things tonight, and there was movement and unrest among the creatures that were wont to sleep through the dark hours. Assuredly there was a disturbing element in the forest, and Ulrich could guess the quarter from whence it came.

He strayed away by himself from the watchers whom he had placed in ambush on the crest of the hill, and wandered far down the steep slopes amid the wild tangle of undergrowth, peering through the tree-trunks and listening through the whistling and skirling of the wind and the restless beating of the branches for sight or sound of the marauders. If only on this wild night, in this dark, lone spot, he might come across Georg Znaeym, man to man, with none to witness—that was the wish that was uppermost in his thoughts. And as he stepped round the trunk of a huge beech, he came face to face with the man he sought.

The two enemies stood glaring at one another for a long silent moment. Each had a rifle in his hand, each had hate in his heart and murder uppermost in his mind. The chance had come to give full play to the passions of a lifetime. But a man who has been brought up under the code of a restraining civilization cannot easily serve himself to shoot down his neighbour in cold blood and without word spoken, except for an offence against his hearth and honour. And before the moment of hesitation had given way to action, a deed of Nature's own violence overwhelmed them both. A fierce shriek of the storm had been answered by a splitting crash over their heads, and ere they could leap aside, a mass of falling beech tree had thundered down on them. Ulrich von Gradwitz found himself stretched on the ground, one arm numb beneath him and the other held almost as helplessly in a tight tangle of forked branches, while both legs were pinned beneath the fallen mass. His heavy shooting-boots had saved his feet from being crushed to pieces, but if his fractures were not as serious as they might have been, at least it was evident that he could not move from his present position till someone came to release him. The descending twigs had slashed the skin of his face, and he had to wink away some drops of blood from his eyelashes before he could take in a general view of the disaster. At his side—so near that under ordinary circumstances he could almost have touched him—lay Georg Znaeym, alive and struggling, but obviously as helplessly pinioned down as himself. All round them lay a thick-strewn wreckage of splintered branches and broken twigs.

Relief at being alive and exasperation at his captive plight brought a strange medley of pious thank-offerings and sharp curses to Ulrich's lips. Georg, who was nearly blinded with the blood which trickled across his eyes, stopped his struggling for a moment to listen, and then gave a short, snarling laugh.

'So you're not killed, as you ought to be but you're caught, anyway,' he cried; 'caught fast. Ho, what a jest, Ulrich von Gradwitz snared in his stolen forest. There's real justice for you!'

And he laughed again, mockingly and savagely.

'I'm caught in my own forest-land,' retorted Ulrich. 'When

my men come to release us you, will wish, perhaps, that you were in a better plight than caught poaching on a neighbour's land, shame on you.'

Georg was silent for a moment; then he answered quietly, 'Are you sure that your men will find much to release? I have men, too, in the forest tonight, close behind me, and they will be here first and do the releasing. When they drag me out from under these damned branches it won't need much clumsiness on their part to roll this mass of trunk right over on the top of you. Your men will find you dead under a fallen beech tree. For form's sake I shall send my condolences to your family.'

'It is a useful hint,' said Ulrich fiercely. 'My men had orders to follow in ten minutes' time, seven of which must have gone by already, and when they get me out—I will remember the hint. Only as you will have met your death poaching on my lands I don't think I can decently send any message of condolence to your family.'

'Good,' snarled Georg, 'good. We fight this quarrel out to the death, you and I and our foresters, with no cursed interlopers to come between us. Death and damnation to you, Ulrich von Gradwitz.'

'The same you, Georg Znaeym, forest-thief, game-snatcher.'

Both men spoke with the bitterness of possible defeat before them, for each knew that it might be long before his men would seek him out or find him; it was a bare matter of chance which party would arrive first on the scene.

Both had now given up the useless struggle to free themselves from the mass of wood that held them down; Ulrich limited his endeavours to an effort to bring his one partially free arm near enough to his outer coat-pocket to draw out his wine-flask. Even when he had accomplished that operation it was long before he could manage the unscrewing of the stopper or get any of the liquid down his throat. But what a Heaven-sent draught it seemed! It was an open winter, and little snow had fallen as yet, hence the captives suffered less from the cold than might have been the case at that season of the year; nevertheless, the wine was warming and reviving to the wounded man, and he looked across with something like a throb of pity to where his enemy lay, just keeping the groans of pain and weariness from crossing his lips.

'Could you reach this flask if I threw it over to you?' asked Ulrich suddenly; 'there is good wine in it, and one may as well be as comfortable as one can. Let us drink, even if tonight one of us dies.'

'No, I can scarcely see anything; there is so much blood caked round my eyes,' said Georg, 'and in any case I don't drink wine with an enemy.'

Ulrich was silent for a few minutes, and lay listening to the weary screeching of the wind. An idea was slowly forming and growing in his brain, an idea that gained strength every time that he looked across at the man who was fighting so grimly against pain and exhaustion. In the pain and languor that Ulrich himself was feeling, the old fierce hatred seemed to be dying down.

'Neighbour,' he said presently, 'do as you please if your men come first. It was a fair compact. But as for me, I've changed my mind. If my men are the first to come, you shall be the first to be helped, as though you were my guest. We have quarrelled like devils all our lives over this stupid strip of forest, where the trees can't even stand upright in a breath of wind. Lying here tonight, I've come to think we've been rather fools; there are better things in life than getting the better of a boundary dispute. Neighbour, if you will help me to bury the old quarrel I—I will ask you to be my friend.'

Georg Znaeym was silent for so long that Ulrich thought, perhaps, he had fainted with the pain of his injuries. Then he spoke slowly and in jerks.

'How the whole region would stare and gabble if we rode into the market-square together. No one living can remember seeing a Znaeym and a von Gradwitz talking to one another in friendship. And what peace there would be among the forester folk if we ended our feud tonight. And if we choose to make peace among our people there is none other to interfere, no interlopers from outside... You would come and keep the Sylvester night beneath my roof, and I would come and feast on some high day at your castle...I would never fire a shot on your land, save when you invited me as a guest; and you should come and shoot with me down in the marshes where the wildfowl are. In all the countryside there are none that could hinder if we willed to make peace. I never thought to have wanted to do other than hate you all my life, but I think I have changed my mind about things too, this last half-hour. And you offered me your wine-flask... Ulrich von Gradwitz, I will be your friend.'

For a space both men were silent, turning over in their minds the wonderful changes that this dramatic reconciliation would bring about. In the cold, gloomy forest, with the wind tearing in fitful gusts through the naked branches and whistling round the tree-trunks, they lay and waited for the help that would now bring release and succour to both parties. And each prayed a private prayer that his men might be the first to arrive, so that he might be the first to show honourable attention to the enemy that had become a friend.

Presently, as the wind dropped for a moment, Ulrich broke silence.

'Let's shout for help,' he said; 'in this lull our voices may carry a little way.'

'They won't carry far through the trees and undergrowth,' said Georg, 'but we can try. Together, then.'

The two raised their voices in a prolonged hunting call.

'Together again,' said Ulrich a few minutes later, after listening in vain for an answering halloo.

'I heard something that time, I think,' said Ulrich. 'I heard nothing but the pestilential wind,' said Georg hoarsely.

There was silence again for some minutes, and then Ulrich gave a joyful cry.

'I can see figures coming through the wood. They are following in the way I came down the hillside.'

Both men raised their voice in as loud a shout as they could muster.

'They hear us! They've stopped. Now they see us. They're running down the hill towards us,' cried Ulrich.

'How many of them are there?' asked Georg.

'I can't see distinctly,' said Ulrich; 'nine or ten.'

'Then they are yours,' said Georg; 'I had only seven out with me.'

'They are making all the speed they can, brave lads,' said Ulrich gladly.

'Are they your men?' asked Georg. 'Are they your men?' he repeated impatiently as Ulrich did not answer.

'No,' said Ulrich with a laugh, the idiotic chattering laugh of a man unstrung with hideous fear.

'Who are they?' asked Georg quickly, straining his eyes to see what the other would gladly not have seen.

'*Wolves*.'

THE MARK OF THE BEAST

Rudyard Kipling

East of Suez, some hold, the direct control of Providence ceases; man being there handed over to the power of the gods and devils of Asia, and the Church of England Providence only exercising an occasional and modified supervision in the case of Englishmen.

This theory accounts for some of the more unnecessary horrors of life in India: it may be stretched to explain my story.

My friend Strickland of the police, who knows as much of natives of India as is good for any man, can bear witness to the facts of the case. Dumoise, our doctor, also saw what Strickland and I saw. The inference which he drew from the evidence was entirely incorrect. He is dead now; he died, in a rather curious manner, which has been elsewhere described.

When Fleete came to India, he owned a little money and some land in the Himalayas, near a place called Dharmsala. Both properties had been left him by an uncle, and he came out to finance them. He was a big, heavy, genial and inoffensive man. His knowledge of natives was, of course, limited, and he complained of the difficulties of the language.

He rode in from his place in the hills to spend New Year in

the station, and he stayed with Strickland. On New Year's Eve there was a big dinner at the club, and the night was excusably wet. When men foregather from the uttermost ends of the Empire, they have a right to be riotous. The Frontier had sent down a contingent o' Catch-'em-Alive-O's who had not seen twenty white faces for a year, and were used to ride fifteen miles to dinner at the next fort at the risk of a Khyberee bullet where their drinks should lie. They profited by their new security, for they tried to play pool with a curled-up hedgehog found in the garden, and one of them carried the marker round the room in his teeth. Half a dozen planters had come in from the south and were talking 'horse' to the Biggest Liar in Asia, who was trying to cap all their stories at once. Everybody was there, and there was a general closing up of ranks and taking stock of our losses in dead or disabled that had fallen during the past year.

It was a very wet night, and I remember that we sang 'Auld Lang Syne' with our feet in the Polo Championship Cup, and our heads among the stars, and swore that we were all dear friends. Then some of us went away and annexed Burma, and some tried to open up the Soudan and were opened up by Fuzzies in that cruel scrub outside Suakim, and some found stars and medals, and some were married, which was bad, and some did other things which were worse, and the others of us stayed in our chains and strove to make money on insufficient experiences.

Fleete began the night with sherry and bitters, drank champagne steadily up to dessert, then raw, rasping Capri with all the strength of whisky, took Benedictine with his coffee, four or five whiskies and sodas to improve his pool strokes, beer and bones at half-past two, winding up with old brandy. Consequently, when he came out, at half-past three in the morning, into fourteen degrees of frost, he was very angry with his horse for coughing, and tried to leapfrog into the saddle. The horse broke away and went to his stables; so Strickland and I formed a Guard of Dishonour to take Fleete home.

Our road lay through the bazaar, close to a little temple of Hanuman, the monkey-god, who is a leading divinity worthy of respect. All gods have good points, just as have all priests. Personally, I attach much importance to Hanuman, and am kind to his people——the great gray apes of the hills. One never knows when one may want a friend.

There was a light in the temple, and as we passed, we could hear voices of men chanting hymns. In a native temple, the priests rise at all hours of the night to do honour to their God. Before we could stop him, Fleete dashed up the steps, patted two priests on the back, and was gravely grinding the ashes of his cigar butt into the forehead of the red stone image of Hanumun. Strickland tried to drag him out, but he sat down and said solemnly:

'Shee that? Mark of the B—beasht! Imade it. Ishn't it fine?'

In half a minute the temple was alive and noisy, and Strickland, who knew what came of polluting gods, said that things might occur. He, by virtue of his official position, long residence in the country, and weakness for going among the natives, was known to the priests and he felt unhappy. Fleete sat on the ground and refused to move. He said that 'good old Hanuman' made a very soft pillow.

Then, without any warning, a Silver Man came out of a recess behind the image of the god. He was perfectly naked in that bitter, bitter cold, and his body shone like frosted silver, for he was what the Bible calls 'a leper as white as snow'. Also, he had no face, because he was a leper of some years' standing and his disease was heavy upon him. We two stooped to haul Fleete up, and the temple was filling and filling with folk who seemed to spring from the earth, when the Silver Man ran in under our arms, making a noise exactly like the mewing of an otter, caught Fleete round the body and dropped his head on Fleete's breast before we could wrench him away. Then he retired to a corner and sat mewing while the crowd blocked all the doors.

The priests were very angry until the Silver Man touched Fleete. That nuzzling seemed to sober them.

At the end of a few minutes' silence one of the priests came to Strickland and said, in perfect English, 'Take your friend away. He was done with Hanuman, but Hanuman has not done with him.' The crowd gave room and we carried Fleete into the road.

Strickland was very angry. He said that we might all three have been knifed, and that Fleete should thank his stars that he had escaped without injury.

Fleete thanked no one. He said that he wanted to go to bed. He was gorgeously drunk.

We moved on, Strickland silent and wrathful, until Fleete was taken with violent shivering fits and sweating. He said that the smells of the bazaar were overpowering, and he wondered why slaughter-houses were permitted so near English residences. 'Can't you smell the blood?' said Fleete.

We put him to bed at last, just as the dawn was breaking, and Strickland invited me to have another whisky and soda. While we were drinking, he talked of the trouble in the temple and admitted that it baffled him completely. Strickland hates being mystified by natives, because his business in life is to overmatch them with their own weapons. He has not yet succeeded in doing this, but in fifteen or twenty years he will have made some small progress.

'They should have mauled us,' he said, 'instead of mewing at us. I wonder what they meant. I don't like it one little bit.'

I said that the Managing Committee of the temple would in all probability bring a criminal action against us for insulting their religion. There was a section of the Indian Penal Code which exactly met Fleete's offense. Strickland said he only hoped and prayed that they would do this. Before I left I looked into Fleete's room and saw him lying on his right side, scratching his left breast. Then I went to bed—cold, depressed, and unhappy—at seven o'clock in the morning.

At one o'clock I rode over to Strickland's house to inquire after Fleete's head. I imagined that it would be a sore one. Fleete was breakfasting and seemed unwell. His temper was gone, for he was abusing the cook for not supplying him with an underdone chop. A man who can eat raw meat after a wet night is a curiosity. I told Fleete this and he laughed.

'You breed queer mosquitoes in these parts,' he said. 'I've been bitten to pieces, but only in one place.'

'Let's have a look at the bite,' said Strickland. 'It may have gone down since this morning.'

While the chops were being cooked, Fleete opened his shirt and showed us, just over his left breast, a mark, the perfect double of the black rosettes—the five or six irregular blotches arranged in a circle—on a leopard's hide. Strickland looked and said, 'It was only pink this morning. It's grown black now.'

Fleete ran to a glass.

'By Jove!' he said, 'this is nasty. What is it?'

We could not answer. Here the chops came in, all red and juicy, and Fleete bolted three in a most offensive manner. He ate on his right grinders only, and threw his head over his right shoulder as he snapped the meat. When he had finished, it struck him that he had been behaving strangely, for he said apologetically, 'I don't think I ever felt so hungry in my life. I've bolted like an ostrich.'

After breakfast Strickland said to me, 'Don't go. Stay here, and stay for the night.'

Seeing that my house was not three miles from Strickland's, this request was absurd. But Strickland insisted, and was going to say something when Fleete interrupted by declaring in a shamefaced way that he felt hungry again. Strickland sent a man to my house to fetch over my bedding and a horse, and we three went down to Strickland's stables to pass the hours until it was time to go out for a ride. The man who has a weakness for horses never wearies of inspecting them; and when two men are killing time in this way, they gather knowledge and lies the one from the other.

There were five horses in the stables, and I shall never forget the scene as we tried to look them over. They seemed to have gone mad. They reared and screamed and nearly tore up their pickets; they sweated and shivered and lathered and were distraught with fear. Strickland's horses used to know him as well as his dogs; which made the matter more curious. We left the stable for fear of the brutes throwing themselves in their panic. Then Strickland turned back and called me. The horses were still frightened, but they let us 'gentle' and make much of them, and put their heads in our bosoms.

'They aren't afraid of us,' said Strickland. 'D'you know, I'd give three months' pay if Outrage here could talk.'

But Outrage was dumb, and could only cuddle up to his master and blow out his nostrils, as is the custom of horses when they wish to explain things but can't. Fleete came up when we were in the stalls, and as soon as the horses saw him, their fright broke out afresh. It was all that we could do to escape from the place unkicked. Strickland said, 'They don't seem to love you, Fleete.'

'Nonsense,' said Fleete; 'my mare will follow me like a

dog,' he went to her; she was in a loose-box; but as he slipped the bars she plunged, knocked him down, and broke away into the garden. I laughed, but Strickland was not amused. He took his moustache in both fists and pulled at it till it nearly came out. Fleete, instead of going off to chase his property, yawned, saying that he felt sleepy. He went to the house to lie down, which was a foolish way of spending New Year's Day.

Strickland sat with me in the stables and asked if I had noticed anything peculiar in Fleete's manner. I said that he ate his food like a beast; but that this might have been the result of living alone in the hills out of the reach of society as refined and elevating as ours for instance. Strickland was not amused. I do not think that he listened to me, for his next sentence referred to the mark on Fleete's breast, and I said that it might have been caused by blister-flies, or that it was possibly a birthmark newly born and now visible for the first time. We both agreed that it was unpleasant to look at, and Strickland found occasion to say that I was a fool.

'I can't tell you what I think now,' said he, 'because you would call me a madman; but you must stay with me for the next few days, if you can. I want you to watch Fleete, but don't tell me what you think till I have made up my mind.'

'But I am dining out tonight,' I said.

'So am I,' said Strickland, 'and so is Fleete. At least if he doesn't change his mind.'

We walked about the garden smoking, but saying nothing—because we were friends, and talking spoils good tobacco—till our pipes were out. Then we went to wake up Fleete. He was wide awake and fidgeting about his room.

'I say, I want some more chops,' he said. 'Can I get them?'

We laughed and said, 'Go and change. The ponies will be round in a minute.'

'All right,' said Fleete. 'I'll go when I get the chops—underdone ones, mind.'

He seemed to be quite in earnest. It was four o'clock, and we had had breakfast at one; still, for a long time, he demanded those underdone chops. Then he changed into riding clothes and went out into the verandah. His pony—the mare had not been caught—would not let him come near. All three horses were unmanageable—mad with fear—and finally Fleete said that he would stay at home and get something to eat. Strickland and I rode out wondering. As we passed the temple of Hanuman, the Silver Man came out and mewed at us.

'He is not one of the regular priests of the temple,' said Strickland. 'I think I should peculiarly like to lay my hands on him.'

There was no spring in our gallop on the racecourse that evening. The horses were stale, and moved as though they had been ridden out.

'The fright after breakfast has been too much for them,' said Strickland.

That was the only remark he made through the remainder of the ride. Once or twice I think he swore to himself; but that did not count.

We came back in the dark at seven o'clock and saw that there were no lights in the bungalow. 'Careless ruffians my servants are!' said Strickland.

My horse reared at something on the carriage drive, and Fleete stood up under its nose.

'What are you doing, grovelling about the garden?' said Strickland.

But both horses bolted and nearly threw us. We dismounted by the stables and returned to Fleete, who was on his hands and knees under the orange bushes.

'What the devil's wrong with you?' said Strickland.

'Nothing, nothing in the world,' said Fleete, speaking very quickly and thickly. 'I've been gardening—botanizing you know. The smell of the earth is delightful. I think I'm going for a walk—a long walk—all night.'

Then I saw that there was something excessively out of order somewhere, and I said to Strickland, 'I am not dining out.'

'Bless you!' said Strickland. 'Here, Fleete, get up. You'll catch fever there. Come in to dinner and let's have the lamps lit. We'll all dine at home.'

Fleete stood up unwillingly, and said, 'No lamps—no lamps. It's much nicer here. Let's dine outside and have some more chops—lots of 'em and underdone—bloody ones with gristle.'

Now a December evening in Northern India is bitterly cold, and Fleete's suggestion was that of a maniac.

'Come in,' said Strickland sternly. 'Come in at once.'

Fleete came, and when the lamps were brought, we saw that he was literally plastered with dirt from head to foot. He must have been rolling in the garden. He shrank from the light and went to his room. His eyes were horrible to look at. There was a green light behind them, not in them, if you understand, and the man's lower lip hung down.

Strickland said, 'There is going to be trouble—big trouble—tonight. Don't change your riding things.'

We waited and waited for Fleete's reappearance, and ordered dinner in the meantime. We could hear him moving about his own room, but there was no light there. Presently, from the room came the long-drawn howl of a wolf.

People write and talk lightly of blood running cold and hair standing up and things of that kind. Both sensations are too horrible to be trifled with. My heart stopped as though a knife had been driven through it; and Strickland turned white as the tablecloth.

The howl was repeated, and was answered by another howl far across the fields.

That set the gilded roof on the horror. Strickland dashed into Fleete's room. I followed, and we saw Fleete getting out of the window. He made beast-noises in the back of his throat. He could not answer us when we shouted at him. He spat.

I don't quite remember what followed, but I think that Strickland must have stunned him with the long boot-jack or else I should never have been able to sit on his chest. Fleete could not speak, he could only snarl, and his snarls were those of a wolf, not of a man. The human spirit must have been giving way all day and have died out with the twilight. We were dealing with a beast that had once been Fleete.

The affair was beyond any human and rational experience. I tried to say 'hydrophobia', but the word wouldn't come, because I knew that I was lying.

We bound this beast with leather thongs of the punkah-rope, and tied its thumbs and big toes together, and gagged it with a shoehorn, which makes a very efficient gag if you know how to arrange it. Then we carried it into the dining room, and sent a man to Dumoise, the doctor, telling him to come over at once. After we had despatched the messenger and were drawing breath, Strickland said, 'It's no good. This isn't any doctor's work.' I, also, knew that he spoke the truth.

The beast's head was free, and it threw it about from side to side. Anyone entering the room would have believed that we were curing a wolf's pelt. That was the most loathsome accessory of all.

Strickland sat with his chin in the heel of his fist, watching the beast as it wriggled on the ground, but saying nothing. The shirt had been torn open in the scuffle and showed the black rosette mark on the left breast. It stood out like a blister.

In the silence of the watching we heard something without, mowing like a she-otter. We both rose to our feet, and—I answer for myself, not Strickland—felt sick—actually and physically sick. We told each other, as did the men in Pinafore, that it was the cat.

Dumoise arrived, and I never saw a little man so unprofessionally shocked. He said that it was a heartrending case of hydrophobia and that nothing could be done. At least, any palliative measures would only prolong the agony. The beast was foaming at the mouth. Fleete, as we told Dumoise, had been bitten by dogs once or twice. Any man who keeps half a dozen terriers must expect a nip now and again. Dumoise could offer no help. He could only certify that Fleete was dying of hydrophobia. The beast was then howling, for it had managed to spit out the shoehorn. Dumoise said that he would be ready to certify to the cause of death, and that the end was certain. He was a good little man, and he offered to remain with us; but Strickland refused the kindness. He did not wish to poison Dumoise's New Year. He would only ask him not to give the real cause of Fleete's death to the public.

So Dumoise left, deeply agitated; and as soon as the noise of the cartwheels had died away, Strickland told me, in a whisper, his suspicions. They were so wildly improbable that he dared not say them out aloud; and I, who entertained all Strickland's beliefs, was so ashamed of owning to them that I pretended to disbelieve.

'Even if the Silver Man had bewitched Fleete for polluting the image of Hanuman, the punishment could not have fallen so quickly.'

As I was whispering this the cry outside the house rose again, and the beast fell into a fresh paroxysm of struggling till we were afraid that the thongs that held it would give way.

'Watch!' said Strickland. 'If this happens six times I shall take the law into my own hands. I order you to help me.'

He went into his room and came out in a few minutes with the barrels of an old shotgun, a piece of fishing-line, some thick cord, and his heavy wooden bedstead. I reported that the convulsions had followed the cry by two seconds in each case, and the beast seemed perceptibly weaker.

Strickland muttered, 'But he can't take away the life! He can't take away the life!'

I said, though I knew that I was arguing against myself, 'It may be a cat. It must be a cat. If the Silver Man is responsible, why does he dare to come here?'

Strickland arranged the wood on the hearth, put the gun barrels into the glow of the fire, spread the twine on the table and broke a walking stick in two. There was one yard of fishing line, gut, lapped with wire, such as is used for mahseer-fishing, and he tied the two ends together in a loop.

Then he said, 'How can we catch him? He must be taken alive and unhurt.'

I said that we must trust in Providence, and go out softly with polo sticks into the shrubbery at the front of the house. The man or animal that made the cry was evidently moving round the house as regularly as a night watchman. We could wait in the bushes till he came by and knock him over.

Strickland accepted this suggestion, and we slipped out from a bathroom window into the front verandah and then across the carriage drive into the bushes.

In the moonlight we could see the leper coming round the corner of the house. He was perfectly naked, and from time to time he mewed and stopped to dance with his shadow. It was an unattractive sight, and thinking of poor Fleete, brought to such degradation by so foul a creature, I put away all my doubts and resolved to help Strickland from the heated gun barrels to the loop of twine—from the loins to the head and back again—with all tortures that might be needful.

The leper halted in the front porch for a moment and we jumped out on him with the sticks. He was wonderfully strong, and we were afraid that he might escape or be fatally injured before we caught him. We had an idea that lepers were frail creatures, but this proved to be incorrect. Strickland knocked his legs from under him and I put my foot on his neck. He mewed hideously, and even through my riding boots I could feel that his flesh was not the flesh of a clean man.

He struck at us with his hand and feet-stumps. We looped the lash of a dog whip round him, under the armpits and dragged him backwards into the hall and so into the dining room where the beast lay. There we tied him with trunk straps. He made no attempt to escape, but mewed.

When we confronted him with the beast, the scene was beyond description. The beast doubled backwards into a bow as though he had been poisoned with strychnine, and moaned in the most pitiable fashion. Several other things happened also, but they cannot be put down here.

'I think I was right,' said Strickland. 'Now, we will ask him to cure this case.'

But the leper only mewed. Strickland wrapped a towel round his hand and took the gun barrels out of the fire. I put the half of the broken walking stick through the loop of fishing-line and buckled the leper comfortably to Strickland's bedstead. I understood then how men and women and little children can endure to see a witch burnt alive; for, the beast was moaning on the floor, and though the Silver Man had no face, you could see horrible feeling passing through the slab that took its place, exactly as waves of heat play across red-hot iron—gun barrels for instance.

Strickland shaded his eyes with his hands for a moment and we got to work. This part is not to be printed.

The dawn was beginning to break when the leper spoke. His mewings had not been satisfactory up to that point. The beast had fainted from exhaustion and the house was very still. We unstrapped the leper and told him to take away the evil spirit. He crawled to the beast and laid his hand upon the left breast. That was all. Then he fell face down and whined, drawing in his breath as he did so.

We watched the face of the beast, and saw the soul of Fleete coming back into the eyes. Then a sweat broke out on the forehead, and the eyes—they were human eyes—closed. We waited for an hour but Fleete still slept. We carried him to his room and bade the leper go, giving him the bedstead and the sheet on the bedstead to cover his nakedness, the gloves and the towels with which we had touched him, and the whip that had been hooked round his body. He put the sheet about him and went out into the early morning without speaking or mewing.

Strickland wiped his face and sat down. A night-gong, far away in the city, made seven o'clock.

'Exactly four-and-twenty hours!' said Strickland. 'And, I've done enough to ensure my dismissal from the service, besides permanent quarters in a lunatic asylum. Do you believe that we are awake?'

The red-hot gun barrel had fallen on the floor and was singeing the carpet. The smell was entirely real.

That morning at eleven we two together went to wake up Fleete. We looked and saw that the black leopard-rosette on his chest had disappeared. He was very drowsy and tired, but as soon as he saw us, he said, 'Oh! Confound you fellows. Happy New Year to you. Never mix your liquors. I'm nearly dead.'

'Thanks for your kindness, but you're over time,' said Strickland. 'Today is the morning of the second. You've slept the clock round with a vengeance.'

The door opened and little Dumoise put his head in. He had come on foot, and fancied that we were laying out Fleete.

'I've brought a nurse,' said Dumoise. 'I suppose that she can come in for what is necessary.'

'By all means,' said Fleete cheerily, sitting up in bed. 'Bring on your nurses,'

Dumoise was dumb. Strickland led him out and explained that there must have been a mistake in the diagnosis. Dumoise remained dumb and left the house hastily. He considered that his professional reputation had been injured, and was inclined to make a personal matter of the recovery. Strickland went out, too. When he came back, he said that he had been to call on the temple of Hanuman to offer redress for the pollution of the god, and had been solemnly assured that no white man had ever touched the idol and that he was an incarnation of all the virtues labouring under a delusion. 'What do you think?' said Strickland.

I said, 'There are more things...'

But Strickland hates that quotation. He says that I have worn it threadbare.

One other curious thing happened which frightened me as much as anything in all the night's work. When Fleete was dressed he came into the dining room and sniffed. He had a quaint trick of moving his nose when he sniffed. 'Horrid doggy smell, here,' said he. 'You should really keep those terriers of yours in better order. Try sulphur, Strick.'

But Strickland did not answer. He caught hold of the back of a chair, and, without warning, went into an amazing fit of hysterics. It is terrible to see a strong man overtaken with hysteria. Then, it struck me that we had fought for Fleete's soul with the Silver Man in that room, and had disgraced ourselves as Englishmen forever, and I laughed and gasped and gurgled just as shamefully as Strickland, while Fleete thought that we had both gone mad. We never told him what we had done.

Some years later, when Strickland had married and was a church-going member of society for his wife's sake, we reviewed the incident dispassionately, and Strickland suggested that I should put it before the public.

I cannot myself see that this step is likely to clear up the mystery; because, in the first place, no one will believe a rather unpleasant story, and, in the second, it is well-known to every right-minded man that the gods of the heathen are stone and brass, and any attempt to deal with them otherwise is justly condemned.

THE WEREWOLF

C.A. Kincaid

It was a terribly hot afternoon in July some fifty years ago in Upper Sind. In the Deccan, cooling showers had turned the hard earth, baked by the summer winds, into a perfect paradise. The soil there was bright with long green grass. The hills rose emerald to the sky, although their summits were often veiled by the monsoon mists; and delightful breezes swept over the glad earth to the great joy of foreign sojourners in the Indian plateau. Even in the Punjab and the Gangetic valley, heavy rain had fallen and if the air seemed stuffy to the traveller from southern India, his eyes rejoiced in the rich foliage and endless maize fields, while his ears listened joyfully to the murmuring sound of newborn streams, as they tinkled and splashed on their way to join the brimming rivers.

In Upper Sind, the landscape was quite different. Rain hardly ever falls there except in the cold weather and while more favoured parts of India revel in the monsoon, none of it reaches that strange land. Irrigated by canals from the Indus, the fields are in winter gay with young wheat and he who visits Upper Sind in January may well think that he has reached some heavenly spot. But let him go there in July or August and he will soon change his opinion. All day long the hot wind roars, driving the mercury up to 120° in the shade; nor is there much relief at night. The hot wind drops, but the thermometer still marks over a hundred; the sandflies and mosquitoes buzz all night and moonbeams like the rays of a powerful electric headlight pour down on the would-be sleeper's face making slumbering exceedingly difficult.

In the middle of this sun-splashed region is Sehwan, formerly an important town, but now greatly sunk in importance. One thing it still claims with justice is that it is one of the hottest places on earth. A Persian poet, once in the bitterness of his heart, asked the Almighty why, after making Sehwan and Sibi, he thought it worthwhile to make Hell. The afternoon on which this story opens was well worthy of Sehwan's ancient reputation. The train steamed slowly into Sehwan station from Sukkur. The railway on the left bank of the Indus had not then been built, so the railtrack passed through Sehwan on its way to Karachi and the seacoast. The last carriage on the train was the saloon of the Traffic Superintendent. It was far roomier than the ordinary first-class carriages, as befitted the quarters of a senior railway official; but nothing could keep out the heat or make the interior cool. The shutters were closed. A railway coolie pulled a diminutive punka fixed on the roof, but he merely stirred into motion the heavy, hot air. There were two occupants of the saloon; one was the Traffic Superintendent, Frank Bollinger; the other was a Major Sinclair, whom he had known for some years. He had invited his friend to share the saloon instead of sweltering in the first-class compartment and sharing it with two missionaries, their wives and baby.

'I shall be devoutly thankful,' said Bollinger, 'when we get out of this Hell into the monsoon area.'

'When will that be?'

'Once we pass the Lakhi gorge it will be better. They say the monsoon dies there and so they call the gorge the gate of Hell. It is true that once past that frightful mass of heated limestone, one does begin to feel a breath of cooler air. It gradually grows in strength; so we ought to get a good night on our way to Karachi.'

'I am very glad to hear that. I could not sleep a wink in this part of the world, could you?'

'Oh! I have had such a long experience of hot nights that I might; but thank God there will be no need to make the experiment.'

Just then, the train drew up in Sehwan station. The stationmaster, Isarmal, who had known Bollinger in earlier days, came running up to pay his respects. His face beamed all over with the pleasure that an Indian almost always feels at meeting a former English friend. Bollinger remembered well the little stationmaster and was also very glad to see him and have a chat over old times.

To let the two old acquaintants have their talk out, Major Sinclair got out of the carriage and strolled about on the platform. After Bollinger and Isarmal had been gossiping together for about a quarter of an hour, the former said suddenly:

'I say, Mr Isarmal, why are we staying here so long? I never remember waiting more than five minutes at Sehwan before.'

'I am afraid, Sir—I am very sorry, Sir—the river has breached the line some four miles down and the train cannot go on until tomorrow morning.'

'Do you mean to say that we shall have to stay all night in this inferno? I am afraid, the Major Sahib will not like that at all. He was grumbling at the heat when the train was moving; what he'll say when he hears that we will have to pass the night in a stationary train, I can't think. He will swear horribly.'

'Yes indeed, Sir,' said Mr Isarmal, anxious to agree to everything his English friend said, 'the Major Sahib will swear horribly.'

Just then all doubts were settled by the arrival of Sinclair in a frightful temper. After so varied an outburst of blasphemy that it filled Bollinger with respectful awe, he shouted:

'Damn it all, Bollinger, have you heard that we have to spend the night in this hellhole?'

'Yes; I'm awfully sorry, old chap; but it cannot be helped. The Indus is in flood and it is just as capricious as a spoilt harlot. Still, it will only be for one night and you'll be able to wipe out your arrears of sleep when we near Karachi.'

'My dear chap, I'm not going to sleep in your saloon. I have just been talking to the khansama of the rest house. He says it is up on the top of a hill and all night one gets a cool breeze from the river. He'll give us dinner and he'll call us at six a.m. so that we shan't miss the train. He'll put our beds out in the open and he swears that we'll be able to sleep like tops.'

Just then the khansama himself came up. He was a powerfully built Panjabi Musulman with a long black beard and very strange yellow eyes. His face in repose had a villainous expression. He had a smile that rarely came off, but it was a very unpleasant one; it was rather like the smile of a savage Alsatian fawning on its master. He could speak a little broken English, which in the case of poor linguists like Major Sinclair was a great attraction. On reaching the saloon he stood at the door and addressing Bollinger very deferentially, said:

'The Major Sahib, he coming to rest house. Sahib, please come, too, and have good night in cool breeze. I give good dinner and you get good sleep and I wake you six a.m. Madras time. Down here too dammed hot, you get no sleep at all, Sahib.'

Bollinger could not help thinking of the old nursery rhyme 'Won't you walk into my parlour said the spider to the fly' and anyway he had no wish to leave his comfortable saloon and a dinner served by his own servants for a hard bed and a doubtful meal at a rest house half a mile away. He politely thanked the khansama.

'No, khansama; I shall be quite all right here. It may be hot, but I doubt whether it will be any cooler on the top of your Himalayan peak. After all, I have been there and it is only about thirty-feet high and my dinner will be better than any you can give me.'

The khansama's yellow eyes flashed disagreeably, but he continued as before to smile in his canine way and to repeat mechanically:

'Sahib, I give you very good dinner. A cool breeze will blow all night. You get good sleep and tomorrow I call you at six a.m. Madras time.'

At last, Bollinger said impatiently: 'It's no use going on jabbering like that. I'm just not going to your rest house. I'm going to stay here and there's an end of it.'

Suddenly, Sinclair broke in: 'Well, I'm not. I'm damned if I'm going to spend the night in your sardine box.' Turning to his butler, he said: 'Here, boy, get my luggage out of the saloon and put it in a tonga and tell the man to drive to the rest house. You can come with the khansama in another.'

Bollinger, taken aback, replied with stiff courtesy: 'My dear Sinclair, you must, of course, please yourself. I shall stay in the old sardine box and you'll have a good dinner and a capital night. Goodnight!'

The Major, without troubling to answer, walked off with the khansama and Bollinger resumed his talk with Mr Isarmal the stationmaster.

When the khansama and Sinclair had passed out of sight Isarmal suddenly said in a low earnest voice: 'Thank God, you did not go, Sahib, with that terrible man. If you had you would be as good as dead already. The Major Sahib will not be alive tomorrow.'

'What on earth are you talking about, Isarmal?'

'It is that khansama, sir. He is not really a man, but a—a—a—I have forgotten the English word; we call it in Sindi a *lakhibaghar*.'

'A hyena, you mean,' said Bollinger, who knew some Sindi.

'Yes, Sahib, he turns himself every night into a hyena and eats anyone whom he finds sleeping alone on a cot in the open. We say that he is the reincarnation of a horrible man called Anu Kasai.'

'Oh, you mean that fellow who ate up Bodlo Bahar?'

'Yes, I see the Sahib knows the story. Bodlo Bahar was the disciple of our great Sehwan saint Lal Shahbaz. One day he disappeared. The following morning one of the saint's disciples saw that the bits of mutton that he was cooking for his dinner were jumping about strangely in his pot. Other disciples had the same tale to tell. So, Lal Shahbaz said: "It must be our Bodlo Bahar," and went to the Governor of Sehwan. He asked from whom they had bought the mutton. They all said, "From the butcher Anu Kasai." Now, this wicked man had once been very prosperous, but he had fallen on evil days; and having no money to buy sheep he used to murder strangers and sell their flesh as mutton. The Governor arrested Anu Kasai and searched his shop and house. They were full of human bones. He had for months escaped punishment, but he was caught when he killed a saint like Bodlo Bahar.'

'How did the Governor punish him?'

'He walled him up in the battlements of Sehwan fort, that

is the hill on which the rest house now stands. As you pass it you can see a sort of hollow in the side of it. That is where they walled up Anu the butcher.'

'But what is this talk of the khansama being his reincarnation?'

'Well, Sahib, he has only been here three or four months and yet several people in the town have disappeared. Whenever they have done so, a large hyena has been seen galloping through Sehwan. Not only that, but two Chota Sahibs (subordinate Europeans) who went to the rest house also have disappeared. The khansama said the same in both cases. They dined and slept outside the rest house, but when he brought the tea next morning they had vanished. We say the khansama turns himself into a hyena and eats them during the night. You will never see the Major Sahib again, I am afraid; but thank God you are here! Still, at night close the doors and windows of your saloon, otherwise that khansama may attack you even here. We always shut ourselves in at night, although it is so hot.'

Bollinger was far too wise to laugh at the stationmaster's story. He did not believe that the khansama and the hyena were the same; but remembering his villainous expression he did think it possible that he was a murderer; and after Isarmal had left he began to wonder what he should do.

At last, he determined to go to the rest house and share the danger, if any, with Sinclair. He had no gun, but he had a long heavy hunting knife that, had it been a bit sharper, would have been a very efficient weapon. He did not bother to take his servant as he did not wish to have him on his hands, too. In the glare of the setting sun he walked alone along the dusty limestone road and then up the steep side of the old fort, now the rest house. He noticed as he walked a depression in the fort wall and said to himself that that must be the place where they walled up Anu Kasai. At last, he reached the top of the old fort.

It formed a plateau and in the centre was the rest house. He arrived just as Sinclair was sitting down to dinner outside the building. It certainly was far cooler than in the station siding, for a cool breeze blew from the river.

'Come along, Bollinger, I am so glad you have come,' said Sinclair cordially. 'You must dine with me. We can get a good night here in the breeze. I say, I'm awfully sorry for having been so grumpy just now. I cannot make out what came over me.'

'Oh, that's all right!' said Bollinger cheerily, wondering secretly what Sinclair would think of Isarmal's tale. The khansama also welcomed Bollinger and made ready a place for him. He then served an excellent dinner and after dinner began to put the two officers' cots outside.

'Oh, don't do that, we shall sleep inside.'

'It will be damned hot, almost as hot as in your saloon below.'

'Oh no, we shall leave the windows open and so get a through draught. The stationmaster tells me that the place is alive with scorpions and that one may well get stung if one sleeps outside.'

Sinclair looked towards the khansama, but he made no objection, so Sinclair said, 'Very well; but it will be so hot that we shall not get a wink of sleep.'

'Oh well, no matter, we'll play picquet until midnight. After that it will cool down sufficiently for us to sleep indoors.'

'Right-o!' said Sinclair gloomily, wishing Bollinger in the infernal regions.

From nine on the two men played cards and Bollinger deliberately played badly so that Sinclair might win and remain interested in the game. The simple device succeeded and Sinclair was so pleased that at eleven p.m. he was still absorbed in the piquet. Just then, someone tried the door, but Bollinger had bolted it. A few seconds later, the khansama appeared at the window in front of which had been fixed wire netting to keep the numerous pigeons from soiling the rooms.

'I have brought iced lemonade for the Sahibs,' said the khansama with an obsequious grin. Bollinger thought that he had never seen any man with such an odious expression and his yellow eyes were twinkling as if with some horrible anticipation.

'All right,' said Sinclair. 'I'll open the door.' He rose, and before Bollinger could stop him he had drawn the bolt. Bollinger pushed him aside and flung his weight against the door. It was too late. A huge paw and the muzzle of a monstrous hyena forced their way through the opening. Bollinger brought his knife down with all his strength on the paw. It was too blunt to cut deeply through the hair, but the blow was a heavy one and numbed the brute's limb. A bloodcurdling growl followed and the paw and snout were withdrawn. Bollinger slammed the door and shot the bolt.

'Thank God, we got the better of that brute. I fancy we're rid of it for the night!'

Hearing a noise he looked round and cried 'By God! We're not!' Through a gap in the netting of one of the windows the hyena had forced its head and in a few seconds would have been in the room. This time, Bollinger decided to use the point and not the edge of his knife. He made a thrust at the brute's throat. It swung its head aside in time to avoid a fatal stab; nevertheless, the knife scored a deep cut in its neck. It gave another bloodcurdling growl, dragged out its head and, with blood streaming from its wound, it raced off laughing in the diabolical way that hyenas do when hurt.

'By Jove! What an escape!' said Sinclair thankfully; 'but I suppose you fight that sort of brute everyday.'

No, thank Heaven, I don't, ' and then Bollinger told Sinclair the stationmaster's story and how, on hearing it, he had come to the rest house to see if his help was needed.

Sinclair went up to Bollinger and shook him cordially by the hand: 'Then, my dear chap, I owe you my life. I cannot say how grateful I feel. I shall never forget your help.'

The other smiled and said: 'Oh, nonsense! You'd have done the same for me. But, I say, didn't you bring your boy with you?'

'Yes, I did. I wonder where he is. I hope to goodness the khansama has not killed him.'

'Well, we had better go and look but we must be very way, for if the hyena killed your boy he'll come back.'

'All right, come along. You've got a knife, haven't you? I am afraid I've got nothing.'

The two men went to the back of the rest house and there they found below a slight slope the dead body of Sinclair's Goanese servant. His throat was completely torn open. The hyena must have crept up noiselessly to the servant's bed and torn out his throat, killing him instantly. Then, it must have again become the khansama and tried to enter the rest house with the iced lemonade.

Sinclair stood sorrowfully by the dead man, who had been many years in his service and to whom he was greatly attached.

'I say, we can't do anything for the poor chap,' said Bollinger, 'so we had better go straight back to the rest house. I have a horrid feeling that the brute is somewhere near, coming back to its kill. By God! There it is!'

He pointed to where a huge striped form was galloping straight for them. The two men ran for the rest house as fast as they could; they only reached it in time through Bollinger throwing his coat at the brute's head and thus gaining a moment's respite.

'I wonder what it will do now,' said Sinclair, but it did

nothing. It went slowly back to the body of the Goanese and began to crunch it up, every now and then breaking into screams of diabolical laughter when its neck hurt it.

'I wish to God I had a gun,' said Bollinger, 'but as we haven't, let's try to get some sleep. One will sit up and watch while the other lies down. I'll sit up first.'

'All right,' said Sinclair, and lying down on one of the cots fell dead asleep in spite of the heat and his servant's death.

Bollinger sat in a chair and tried as best he could to keep awake. Still, he must have dropped off for a minute or so, for waking up with a start he saw in the bright moonlight the baleful glare of the hyena's eyes as it stared at him through the wire netting. He drew his knife and ran with a shout towards the netting but the hyena with a growl of fury jumped back and galloped off.

Sinclair woke and hearing what had happened said: 'We must both sit up, otherwise the brute will return and get us.'

The two friends sat and smoked and talked through the weary hours until about 5.30 a.m. when their troubles came to an end. A crowd of Sindis, led by Isarmal, came to the rest house to see what had happened to the two Englishmen.

'God be praised!' exclaimed Isarmal earnestly. 'Nothing has happened and you are both safe!'

'We are safe, but look at this,' and Bollinger led the crowd of Sindis to the half-eaten remains of the unfortunate Goanese: 'The khansama killed him!'

Isarmal's face grew grim and turning to the rest of the crowd he cried: 'Brothers, we are Sindis. The khansama is a Panjabi and therefore, of a race that we hate. He is clearly the reincarnation of Anu Kasai. When the train has gone we must deal with him.'

The two Englishmen walked back with Isarmal to the

station, where the train was standing; as they walked, Bollinger related the events of the night. Afterwards, Isarmal repeated the story in Sindi to the men following him. On reaching the saloon nothing more was said. The two weary travellers got in and Isarmal, as he waved on the train, turned to the Sindis, who were mostly Musulmans, and cried: 'The Sahibs are safe, *Alhamdalilla* (God be praised)!'

After a hot, slow journey the Englishmen reached Karachi. On the way Bollinger said: 'I fancy the khansama has had a bad quarter of an hour. He is a Panjabi and, as Isarmal said, of a race hated by the Sindis.'

'But why do the Sindis hate the Panjabis? I like them.'

'I really do not quite know. Perhaps, like French and Germans Sindis and Panjabis live too near together. The Panjabis, too, are bigger men as a rule than the Sindis and they throw their weight about. The Sindis seem very much afraid of them. Indeed I remember hearing a Sindi proverb that says: "If one Panjabi comes, sit still and say nothing. If two come, then pack up your kit at once, abandon your house and clear out." Anyway, Panjabis are not liked in these parts.'

'They don't seem to be!'

Two mornings after their arrival Davidson, the District Superintendent of Police, burst unceremoniously into Bollinger's bungalow and onto the verandah, where he was having his chota hazri or morning tea.

'I'm sorry, Bollinger, but I must see you. I have just received an official report from the Chief Constable of Sehwan to the effect that the villagers, led by the stationmaster, broke into the khansama's house, dragged him out although he was very ill and walled him into the battlements of the old fort. He hints that you know something about it. In the meantime, he has arrested the stationmaster, Isarmal I think he calls him.'

'Half a mo', Davidson! I fancy I have a letter from the stationmaster in my morning post. I'll open it.' Tearing open the envelope, Bollinger read aloud the following note, very short and quaintly expressed:

Honoured Sir,

The Chief Constable of Sehwan, who is a Panjabi, is troubling us because of the death of that Anu Kasai, the khansama. After Your Honour's departure we went to his house and found him very ill from a severe wound in the throat. We found in his house the property of the two missing Chota Sahibs; seeing this he became very obstinate and refused to answer our questions. Very soon he died. When dead, we put him where Anu Kasai was walled up. The Sahib knows the facts and will kindly do the needful.

'Well, Bollinger, he says you know the facts, for goodness sake let me have them.'

Bollinger told the full story of the adventure and Sinclair supported him in every detail. Still, as told in an Englishman's house in Karachi, it did not sound very convincing.

'Hang it all, Bollinger! You can't expect me to believe this tale of a werewolf.'

'Well, Isarmal says that they found in the khansama's house the property of those two missing subordinates. That raises a presumption that he is a murderer, anyway.'

'The Chief Constable says nothing about that.'

'He is a brother Panjabi and can scarcely be expected to. Look here, instead of arguing, let's go off and call on the Commissioner. He is Inspector-General of Police, as well as of everything else and we'll abide by his orders.'

'Right-o!' said the District Superintendent and at eleven a.m.

all three men met to call on Government House.

The Commissioner was a big genial man who combined with a very cordial manner a vast amount of common sense. He greeted all three men pleasantly. Then, he turned to the D.S.R. who was in uniform:

'Well, Davidson, what's the trouble?'

'I think, Sir, Bollinger had better tell you his yarn first and then I'll supplement it with my information.'

'Capital! Go ahead, Bollinger.'

The railway man repeated his story and Sinclair confirmed it. Then, Davidson showed the Commissioner his Chief Constable's report and Bollinger produced Isarmal's letter.

The Commissioner's keen intellect grasped immediately all the facts and came at once to a decision.

'Look here, Bollinger, you can't expect me to accept as gospel your story of the werewolf or werehyena; but the khansama seems to have been a murderer all right. The discovery in his house of the property of the two subordinates points to that. I have often been worried as to what became of them. Again, I do not see why we should not believe Isarmal's statement that they did not wall in the khansama until he was dead. Anyway, it will be impossible to disprove it; for all the eyewitnesses will support Isarmal. In any case, if you go into the witness box, Bollinger, and tell your adventure with the khansama-cum-hyena, my administration will be the laughing stock of all India. Think how the young lions of the *Pioneer* will sharpen their wit at our expense. No! No, we must stop the prosecution at all costs. Look here, Davidson, you wire to the Chief Constable to drop the case and release Isarmal and any others he may have arrested; I shall myself transfer to some other district the Chief Constable; for he seems to have been very slack over the disappearance of the two subordinates. Well, good morning.'

Isarmal was duly released and resumed his duties as stationmaster. But Bollinger did not forget him. Using his influence with the railway chiefs, he got Isarmal first promoted to be stationmaster of Radhan and then of Sukkur, a very important post. This Isarmal retained until his retirement. He lived for many years on an ample pension and nothing gave him greater pleasure than to tell the story of the Panjabi who could turn himself into a hyena and how he nearly ate up the two Sahibs. He gave ample credit to Bollinger Sahib for his courage and resource; but the person for whom he reserved the fullest commendation was none other than Mr Isarmal, late stationmaster of Sukkur.

THE BEAST WITH FIVE FINGERS

W.F. Harvey

The story, I suppose, begins with Adrian Borlsover, whom I met when I was a little boy and he an old man. My father had called to appeal for a subscription, and before he left, Mr Borlsover laid his right hand in blessing on my head. I shall never forget the awe in which I gazed up at his face and realized for the first time that eyes might be dark and beautiful and shining, and yet not able to see.

For Adrian Borlsover was blind.

He was an extraordinary man, who came of an eccentric stock. Borlsover sons for some reason always seemed to marry very ordinary women, which perhaps accounted for the fact that no Borlsover had been a genius, and only one Borlsover had been mad. But they were great champions of little causes, generous patrons of odd sciences, founders of querulous sects, trustworthy guides to the bypath meadows of erudition.

Adrian was an authority on the fertilization of orchids. He had held at one time the family living at Borlsover Conyers, until a congenital weakness of the lungs obliged him to seek a less rigorous climate in the sunny south-coast watering-place where I had seen him. Occasionally, he would relieve one or other of the local clergy. My father described him as a fine preacher, who gave long and inspiring sermons from what many men would have considered unprofitable texts. 'An excellent proof,' he would add, 'of the truth of the doctrine of direct verbal inspiration.'

Adrian Borlsover was exceedingly clever with his hands. His penmanship was exquisite. He illustrated all his scientific papers, made his own woodcuts, and carved the reredos that is at present the chief feature of interest in the church at Borlsover Conyers. He had an exceedingly clever knack in cutting silhouettes for young ladies and paper pigs and cows for little children, and made more than one complicated wind instrument of his own devising.

When he was fifty years old, Adrian Borlsover lost his sight. In a wonderfully short time he adapted himself to the new conditions of life. He quickly learnt to read Braille. So marvellous indeed was his sense of touch, that he was still able to maintain his interest in botany. The mere passing of his long supple fingers over a flower was sufficient means for its identification, though occasionally he would use his lips. I have found several letters of his among my father's correspondence; in no case was there anything to show that he was afflicted with blindness, and this in spite of the fact that he exercised undue economy in the spacing of lines. Towards the close of his life, Adrian Borlsover was credited with the powers of touch that seemed almost uncanny. It has been said that he could tell at once the colour of a ribbon placed between his fingers. My father would neither confirm nor deny the story.

Adrian Borlsover was a bachelor. His elder brother, Charles, had married late in life, leaving one son, Eustace, who lived in the gloomy Georgian mansion at Borlsover Conyers, where he could work undisturbed in collecting material for his great book on heredity.

Like his uncle, he was a remarkable man. The Borlsovers had always been born naturalists, but Eustace possessed in a special degree the power of systematizing his knowledge. He had received his university education in Germany; and then, after post-graduate work in Vienna and Naples, had travelled for four years in South America and the East, getting together a huge store of material for a new study into the processes of variation.

He lived alone at Borlsover Conyers with Saunders, his secretary, a man who bore a somewhat dubious reputation in the district, but whose powers as a mathematician, combined with his business abilities, were invaluable to Eustace.

Uncle and nephew saw little of each other. The visits of Eustace were confined to a week in the summer or autumn— tedious weeks, that dragged almost as slowly as the bath-chair in which the old man was drawn along the sunny sea-front. In their way the two men were fond of each other, though their intimacy would, doubtless, have been greater, had they shared the same religious views. Adrian held to the old-fashioned evangelical dogmas of his early manhood; his nephew for many years had been thinking of embracing Buddhism. Both men possessed, too, the reticence the Borlsovers had always shown, and which their enemies sometimes called hypocrisy. With Adrian it was a reticence as to the things he had left undone; but with Eustace it seemed that the curtain which he was so careful to leave undrawn hid something more than a half-empty chamber.

Two years before his death, Adrian Borlsover developed, unknown to himself, the not uncommon power of automatic writing. Eustace made the discovery by accident. Adrian was sitting reading in bed, the forefinger of his left hand tracing the Braille characters, when his nephew noticed that a pencil the old man held in his right hand was moving slowly along the opposite page. He left his seat in the window and sat down beside the bed. The right hand continued to move, and now he could see plainly that they were letters and words which it was forming.

'Adrian Borlsover,' wrote the hand, 'Eustace Borlsover, Charles Borlsover, Francis Borlsover, Sigismund Borlsover, Adrian Borlsover, Eustace Borlsover, Saville Borlsover. B for Borlsover. Honesty is the Best Policy. Beautiful Belinda Borlsover.'

'What curious nonsense!' said Eustace to himself.

'King George ascended the throne in 1760,' wrote the hand. 'Crowd, a noun of multitude; a collection of individuals. Adrian Borlsover, Eustace Borlsover.'

'It seems to me,' said his uncle, closing the book, 'that you had much better make the most of the afternoon sunshine and take your walk now.'

'I think perhaps I will,' Eustace answered as he picked up the volume. 'I won't go far, and when I come back, I can read to you those articles in *Nature* about which we were speaking.'

He went along the promenade, but stopped at the first shelter, and, seating himself in the corner best protected from the wind, he examined the book at leisure. Nearly every page was scored with a meaningless jumble of pencil-marks; rows of capital letters, short words, long words, complete sentences, copy-book tags. The whole thing, in fact had the appearance of a copy-book, and, on a more careful scrutiny, Eustace thought that there was ample evidence to show that the handwriting at the beginning of the book, good though it was, was not nearly so good as the handwriting at the end.

He left his uncle at the end of October with a promise to return early in December. It seemed to him quite clear that the old man's power of automatic writing was developing rapidly, and for the first time he looked forward to a visit that would combine duty with interest.

But on his return he was at first disappointed. His uncle, he thought, looked older. He was listless, too, preferring others to read to him and dictating nearly all his letters. Not until the day before he left had Eustace an opportunity of observing Adrian Borlsover's new-found faculty.

The old man, propped up in bed with pillows, had sunk into a light sleep. His two hands lay on the coverlet, his left hand tightly clasping his right. Eustace took an empty manuscript-book and placed a pencil within reach of the fingers of the right hand. They snatched at it eagerly, then dropped the pencil to loose the left hand from its restraining grasp.

'Perhaps to prevent interference I had better hold that hand,' said Eustace to himself, as he watched the pencil. Almost immediately it began to write.

'Blundering Borlsovers, unnecessarily unnatural, extraordinarily eccentric, culpably curious.'

'Who are you?' asked Eustace in a low voice.

'Never you mind,' wrote the hand of Adrian.

'Is it my uncle who is writing?'

'O my prophetic soul, mine uncle!'

'Is it anyone I know?'

'Silly Eustace, you'll see me very soon.'

'When shall I see you?'

'When poor old Adrian's dead.'

'Where shall I see you?'

'Where shall you not?'

Instead of speaking his next question, Eustace wrote it. 'What is the time?'

The fingers dropped the pencil and moved three or four times across the paper. Then, picking up the pencil, they wrote: 'Ten minutes before four. Put your book away, Eustace. Adrian mustn't find us working at this sort of thing. He doesn't know what to make of it, and I won't have poor old Adrian disturbed. Au revoir!'

Adrian Borlsover awoke with a start.

'I've been dreaming again,' he said; 'such queer dreams of leaguered cities and forgotten towns. You were mixed up in this one, Eustace, though I can't remember how. Eustace, I want to warn you. Don't walk in doubtful paths. Choose your friends well. Your poor grandfather...'

A fit of coughing put an end to what he was saying, but Eustace saw that the hand was still writing. He managed unnoticed to draw the book away. 'I'll light the gas,' he said, 'and ring for tea.' On the other side of the bed-curtain he saw the last sentences that had been written.

'It's too late, Adrian,' he read. 'We're friends already, aren't we, Eustace Borlsover?'

On the following day Eustace left. He thought his uncle looked ill when he said goodbye, and the old man spoke despondently of the failure his life had been.

'Nonsense, uncle,' said his nephew. 'You have got over your difficulties in a way not one in a hundred thousand would have done. Everyone marvels at your splendid perseverance in teaching your hand to take the place of your lost sight. To me it's been a revelation of the possibilities of education.'

'Education,' said his uncle dreamily, as if the word had started a new train of thought. 'Education is good so long as you know to whom and for what purpose you give it. But with the lower orders of men, the base and more sordid spirits, I have grave doubts as to its results. Well, goodbye, Eustace; I may not see you again. You are a true Borlsover, with all the Borlsover faults. Marry, Eustace. Marry some good, sensible girl. And if by any chance I don't see you again, my will is at my solicitor's. I've not left you any legacy, because I know you're well-provided for; but I thought you might like to have my books. Oh, and there's just one other thing. You know, before the end people often lose control over themselves and make absurd requests. Don't pay any attention to them, Eustace. Goodbye!' and he held out his hand. Eustace took it. It remained in his a fraction of a second longer than he had expected and gripped him with a virility that was surprising. There was, too, in its touch a subtle sense of intimacy.

'Why, uncle,' he said, 'I shall see you alive and well for many long years to come.'

Two months later Adrian Borlsover died.

Eustace Borlsover was in Naples at the time. He read the obituary notice in the *Morning Post* on the day announced for the funeral.

'Poor old fellow!' he said. 'I wonder whether I shall find room for all his books.'

The question occurred to him again with greater force when three days later, he found himself standing in the library at Borlsover Conyers, a huge room built for use and not for beauty in the year of Waterloo by a Borlsover who was an ardent admirer of the great Napoleon. It was arranged on the plan of many college libraries, with tall projecting bookcases forming deep recesses of dusty silence, fit graves for the old hates of forgotten controversy, the dead passions of forgotten lives. At the end of the room, behind the bust of some unknown eighteenth-century divine, an ugly iron corkscrew stair led to a shelf-lined gallery. Nearly, every shelf was full.

'I must talk to Saunders about it,' said Eustace. 'I suppose that we shall have to have the billiard-room fitted up with bookcases.'

The two men met for the first time after many weeks in

the dining-room that evening.

'Hallo!' said Eustace, standing before the fire with his hands in his pockets. 'How goes the world, Saunders? Why these dress togs?' He himself was wearing an old shooting-jacket. He did not believe in mourning, as he had told his uncle on his last visit; and, though he usually went in for quiet-coloured ties, he wore this evening one of an ugly red, in order to shock Morton, the butler, and to make them thrash out the whole question of mourning for themselves in the servants' hall. Eustace was a true Borlsover. 'The world,' said Saunders, 'goes the same as usual, confoundedly slow. The dress togs are accounted for by an invitation from Captain Lockwood to bridge.'

'How are you getting there?'

'There's something the matter with the car, so I've told Jackson to drive me round in the dogcart. Any objection?'

'O dear me, no! We've had all things in common for far too many years for me to raise objections at this hour of the day.'

'You'll find your correspondence in the library,' went on Saunders. 'Most of it I've seen to. There are a few private letters I haven't opened. There's also a box with a rat or something inside it that came by the evening post. Very likely it's the six-toed beast Terry was sending us to cross with the four-toed albino. I didn't look because I didn't want to mess up my things; but I should gather from the way it's jumping about that it's pretty hungry'

'Oh, I'll see to it,' said Eustace, 'while you and the captain earn an honest penny.'

Dinner over and Saunders gone, Eustace went into the library. Though the fire had been lit, the room was by no means cheerful.

'We'll have all the lights on, at any rate,' he said, as he turned the switches. 'And, Morton,' he added, when the butler brought the coffee, 'get me a screwdriver or something to undo this box. Whatever the animal is, he's kicking up the deuce of a row. What is it? Why are you dawdling?'

'If you please, sir, when the postman brought it, he told me that they'd bored the holes in the lid at the post office. There were no breathing holes in the lid, sir, and they didn't want the animal to die. That is all, sir.'

'It's culpably careless of the man, whoever he was,' said Eustace as he removed the screws, 'packing an animal like this in a wooden box with no means of getting air. Confound it all! I meant to ask Morton to bring me a cage to put it in. Now I suppose I shall have to get one myself.'

He placed a heavy book on the lid from which the screws had been removed, and went into the billiard-room. As he came back into the library with an empty cage in his hand, he heard the sound of something falling, and then of something scuttling along the floor.

'Bother it! The beast's got out. How in the world am I to find it again in this library?'

To search for it did indeed seem hopeless. He tried to follow the sound of the scuttling in one of the recesses, where the animal seemed to be running behind the books on the shelves; but it was impossible to locate it. Eustace resolved to go on quietly reading. Very likely the animal might gain confidence and show itself. Saunders seemed to have dealt in his usual methodical manner with most of the correspondence. There were still the private letters.

What was that? Two sharp clicks and the lights in the hideous candelabra that hung from the ceiling suddenly went out.

'I wonder if something has gone wrong with the fuse,' said Eustace, as he went to the switches by the door. Then he stopped. There was a noise at the other end of the room, as if something was crawling up the iron corkscrew stair. 'If it's gone into the gallery,' he said, 'well and good.' He hastily turned on the lights, crossed the room, and climbed up the stair. But he could see nothing. His grandfather had placed a little gate at the top of the stair, so that children could run and romp in the gallery without fear of accident. This Eustace closed, and, having considerably narrowed the circle of his search, returned to his desk by the fire.

How gloomy the library was! There was no sense of intimacy about the room. The few busts that an eighteenth-century Borlsover had brought back from the grand tour might have been in keeping in the old library. Here they seemed out of place. They made the room feel cold in spite of the heavy red damask curtains and great gilt cornices.

With a crash two heavy books fell from the gallery to the floor; then, as Borlsover looked, another, and yet another.

'Very well. You'll starve for this, my beauty!' he said. 'We'll do some little experiments on the metabolism of rats deprived of water. Go on! Chuck them down! I think I've got the upper hand.' He turned once more to his correspondence. The letter was from the family solicitor. It spoke of his uncle's death, and of the valuable collection of books that had been left to him in the will.

'There was one request [he read] which certainly came as a surprise to me. As you know, Mr Adrian Borlsover had left instructions that his body was to be buried in as simple a manner as possible at Eastbourne. He expressed a desire that there should be neither wreaths nor flowers of any kind, and hoped that his friends and relatives would not consider it necessary to wear mourning. The day before his death we received a letter cancelling these instructions. He wished the body to be embalmed (he gave us the address of the man we were to employ—Pennifer, Ludgate Hill), with orders that his right hand should be sent to you stating that it was at your special request. The other arrangements about the funeral remained unaltered.'

'Good Lord,' said Eustace, 'what in the world was the old boy driving at? And what in the name of all that's holy is that?'

Someone was in the gallery. Someone had pulled the cord attached to one of the blinds, and it had rolled up with a snap. Someone must be in the gallery, for a second blind did the same. Someone must be walking round the gallery, for one after the other the blinds sprang up, letting in the moonlight.

'I haven't got to the bottom of this yet,' said Eustace, 'but I will do, before the night is very much older'; and he hurried up the corkscrew stair. He had just got to the top when the lights went out a second time, and he heard again the scuttling along the floor. Quickly he stole on tiptoe in the dim moonshine in the direction of the noise, feeling, as he went, for one of the switches. His fingers touched the metal knob at last. He turned on the electric light.

About ten yards in front of him, crawling along the floor, was a man's hand. Eustace stared at it in utter amazement. It was moving quickly in the manner of a geometer caterpillar, the fingers humped up one moment, flattened out the next; the thumb appeared to give a crablike motion all the while. While he was looking, too surprised to stir, the hand disappeared round the corner. Eustace ran forward. He no longer saw it, but he could hear it, as it squeezed its way behind the books on one of the shelves. A heavy volume had been displaced. There was a gap in the row of books, where it had got in. In his fear lest it should escape him again, he seized the first book that came to his hand and plugged it into the hole. Then, emptying two shelves of their contents, he took the wooden boards and propped them up in front to make his barrier doubly sure.

'I wish Saunders was back,' he said; 'one can't tackle this sort of thing alone.' It was after eleven, and there seemed little likelihood of Saunders returning before twelve. He did not dare to leave the shelf unwatched, even to run downstairs to ring the bell. Morton, the butler, often used to come round about eleven to see that the windows were fastened, but he might not come. Eustace was thoroughly unstrung. At last he heard steps down below.

'Morton!' he shouted. 'Morton!'

'Sir?'

'Has Mr Saunders got back yet?'

'Not yet, sir.'

'Well, bring me some brandy, and hurry up about it. I'm up in the gallery, you duffer.'

'Thanks,' said Eustace, as he emptied the glass. 'Don't go to bed yet, Morton. There are a lot of books that have fallen down by accident. Bring them up and put them back on their shelves.'

Morton had never seen Borlsover in so talkative a mood as on that night. 'Here,' said Eustace, when the books had been put back and dusted, 'you might hold up these boards for me, Morton. That beast in the box got out, and I've been chasing it all over the place.'

'I think I can hear it chewing at the books, sir. They're not valuable, I hope? I think that's the carriage, sir; I'll go and call Mr Saunders.'

It seemed to Eustace that he was away for five minutes, but it could hardly have been more than one, when he returned with Saunders. 'All right, Morton, you can go now. I'm up here, Saunders.'

'What's all the row?' asked Saunders, as he lounged forward

with his hands in his pockets. The luck had been with him all the evening. He was completely satisfied, both with himself and with Captain Lockwood's taste in wines. 'What's the matter? You look to me to be in an absolutely blue funk.'

'That old devil of an uncle of mine,' began Eustace—'Oh, I can't explain it all. It's his hand that's been playing Old Harry all the evening. But I've got it cornered behind these books. You've got to help me to catch it.'

'What's up with you, Eustace? What's the game?'

'It's no game, you silly idiot! If you don't believe me, take out one of those books and put your hand in and feel.'

'All right,' said Saunders; 'but wait till I've rolled up my sleeve. The accumulated dust of centuries, eh?' He took off his coat, knelt down, and thrust his arm along the shelf.

'There's something there right enough,' he said. 'It's got a funny, stumpy end to it, whatever it is, and nips like a crab. Ah! no, you don't!' He pulled his hand out in a flash. 'Shove in a book quickly. Now it can't get out.'

'What was it?' asked Eustace.

'Something that wanted very much to get hold of me. I felt what seemed like a thumb and forefinger. Give me some brandy.'

'How are we to get it out of there?'

'What about a landing-net?'

'No good. It would be too smart for us. I tell you, Saunders, it can cover the ground far faster than I can walk. But I think I see how we can manage it. The two books at the end of the shelf are big ones, that go right back against the wall. The others are very thin. I'll take out one at a time, and you slide the rest along, until we have it squashed between the end two.'

It certainly seemed to be the best plan. One by one as they took out the books, the space behind grew smaller and smaller. There was something in it that was certainly very much alive.

Once they caught sight of fingers feeling for a way of escape. At last they had it pressed between the two big books.

'There's muscle there, if there isn't warm flesh and blood,' said Saunders, as he held them together. 'It seems to be a hand right enough, too. I suppose this is a sort of infectious hallucination. I've read about such cases before.'

'Infectious fiddlesticks!' said Eustace, his face white with anger; 'bring the thing downstairs. We'll get it back into the box.'

It was not altogether easy, but they were successful at last. 'Drive in the screws,' said Eustace; 'we won't run any risks. Put the box in this old desk of mine. There's nothing in it that I want. Here's the key. Thank goodness there's nothing wrong with the lock.'

'Quite a lively evening,' said Saunders. 'Now let's hear more about your uncle.'

They sat up together until early morning. Saunders had no desire for sleep. Eustace was trying to explain and to forget; to conceal from himself a fear that he had never felt before—the fear of walking alone down the long corridor to his bedroom.

'Whatever it was,' said Eustace to Saunders on the following morning, 'I propose that we drop the subject. There's nothing to keep us here for the next ten days. We'll motor up to the Lakes and get some climbing.'

'And see nobody all day, and sit bored to death with each other every night. Not for me, thanks. Why not run up to town? Run's the exact word in this case, isn't it? We're both in such a blessed funk. Pull yourself together, Eustace, and let's have another look at the hand.'

'As you like,' said Eustace; 'there's the key.'

They went into the library and opened the desk. The box was as they had left it on the previous night.

'What are you waiting for?' asked Eustace.

'I am waiting for you to volunteer to open the lid. However since you seem to funk it, allow me. There doesn't seem to be the likelihood of any rumpus this morning at all events.' He opened the lid and picked out the hand.

'Cold?' asked Eustace.

'Tepid. A bit below blood heat by the feel. Soft and supple too. If it's the embalming, it's a sort of embalming I've never seen before. Is it your uncle's hand?'

'Oh yes, it's his all right,' said Eustace. 'I should know those long thin fingers anywhere. Put it back in the box, Saunders. Never mind about the screws. I'll lock the desk, so that there'll be no chance of its getting out. We'll compromise by motoring up to town for a week. If we can get off soon after lunch, we ought to be at Grantham or Stamford by night.'

'Right,' said Saunders, 'and tomorrow—oh, well, by tomorrow we shall have forgotten all about this beastly thing.'

If, when the morrow came, they had not forgotten, it was certainly true that at the end of the week they were able to tell a very vivid ghost-story at the little supper Eustace gave on Halloween.

'You don't want us to believe that it's true, Mr Borlsover? How perfectly awful!'

'I'll take my oath on it, and so would Saunders here; wouldn't you, old chap?'

'Any number of oaths,' said Saunders. 'It was a long thin hand, you know, and it gripped me just like that.'

'Don't, Mr Saunders! Don't! How perfectly horrid! Now tell us another one, do! Only a really creepy one, please.'

'Here's a pretty mess!' said Eustace on the following day, as he threw a letter across the table to Saunders. 'It's your affair, though. Mrs Merrit, if I understand it, gives a month's notice.'

'Oh, that's quite absurd on Mrs Merrit's part,' replied

Saunders. 'She doesn't know what she's talking about. Let's see what she says.'

> Dear Sir [he read]. This is to let you know that I must give you a month's notice as from Tuesday, the 13th. For a long time I've felt the place too big for me; but when Jane Parfit and Emma Laidlaw go off with scarcely as much as an "If you please", after frightening the wits out of the other girls, so that they can't turn out a room by themselves or walk alone down the stairs for fear of treading on half-frozen toads or hearing it run along the passages at night, all I can say is that it's no place for me. So I must ask you, Mr Borlsover, sir, to find a new housekeeper, that has no objection to large and lonely houses, which some people do say, not that I believe them for a minute, my poor mother always having been a Wesleyan, are haunted.
>
> Yours faithfully,
>
> Elizabeth Merrit.
>
> PS.—I should be obliged if you would give my respects to Mr Saunders. I hope that he won't run any risks with his cold.

'Saunders,' said Eustace, 'you've always had a wonderful way with you in dealing with servants. You mustn't let poor old Merrit go.'

'Of course she shan't go,' said Saunders. 'She's probably only angling for a rise in salary. I'll write to her this morning.'

'No. There's nothing like a personal interview. We've had enough of town. We'll go back tomorrow, and you must work your cold for all it's worth. Don't forget that it's got on to the chest, and will require weeks of feeding up and nursing.'

'All right; I think I can manage Mrs Merrit.'

But Mrs Merrit was more obstinate than he had thought. She was very sorry to hear of Mr Saunders's cold, and how he lay awake all night in London coughing; very sorry indeed. She'd change his room for him, gladly, and get the south room aired, and wouldn't he have a hot basin of bread and milk last thing at night? But she was afraid that she would have to leave at the end of the month.

'Try her with an increase of salary,' was the advice of Eustace.

It was no use. Mrs Merrit was obdurate, though she knew of a Mrs Goddard, who had been housekeeper to Lord Gargrave, who might be glad to come at the salary mentioned.

'What's the matter with the servants, Morton?' asked Eustace that evening, when he brought the coffee into the library. 'What's all this about Mrs Merrit wanting to leave?'

'If you please, sir, I was going to mention it myself. I have a confession to make, sir. When I found your note, asking me to open that desk and take out the box with the rat, I broke the lock, as you told me, and was glad to do it, because I could hear the animal in the box making a great noise, and I thought it wanted food. So I took out the box, sir, and got a cage, and was going to transfer it, when the animal got away.'

'What in the world are you talking about? I never wrote any such note.'

'Excuse me, sir; it was the note I picked up here on the floor on the day you and Mr Saunders left. I have it in my pocket now.'

It certainly seemed to be in Eustace's handwriting. It was written in pencil, and began somewhat abruptly.

'Get a hammer, Morton,' he read, 'or some other tool and break open the lock in the old desk in the library. Take out the box that is inside. You need not do anything else. The lid is already open. Eustace Borlsover.'

'And you opened the desk?'

'Yes, sir; and, as I was getting the cage ready, the animal hopped out.'

'What animal?'

'The animal inside the box, sir.'

'What did it look like?'

'Well, sir, I couldn't tell you,' said Morton nervously. 'My back was turned, and it was halfway down the room when I looked up.'

'What was its colour?' asked Saunders. 'Black?'

'Oh no, sir; a greyish white. It crept along in a very funny way, sir. I don't think it had a tail.'

'What did you do then?'

'I tried to catch it; but it was no use. So I set the rat-traps and kept the library shut. Then that girl, Emma Laidlaw, left the door open when she was cleaning, and I think it must have escaped.'

And you think it is the animal that's been frightening the maids?'

'Well, no sir, not quite. They said it was—you'll excuse me sir—a hand that they saw. Emma trod on it once at the bottom of the stairs. She thought then it was a half-frozen toad, only white. And then Parfit was washing up the dishes in the scullery. She wasn't thinking about anything in particular. It was close on dusk. She took her hands out of the water and was drying them absent-minded like on the roller towel, when she found she was drying someone else's hand as well, only colder than hers.'

'What nonsense!' exclaimed Saunders.

'Exactly sir; that's what I told her; but we couldn't get her to stop.'

'You don't believe all this?' said Eustace, turning suddenly towards the butler.

'Me, sir? Oh no, sir! I've not seen anything.'

'Nor heard anything?'

'Well, sir, if you must know, the bells do ring at odd times, and there's nobody there when we go; and when we go round to draw the blinds of a night, as often as not somebody's been there before us. But, as I says to Mrs Merrit, a young monkey might do wonderful things, and we all know that Mr Borlsover has had some strange animals about the place.'

'Very well, Morton, that will do.'

'What do you make of it?' asked Saunders, when they were alone. 'I mean of the letter he said you wrote.'

'Oh, that's simple enough,' said Eustace. 'See the paper it's written on? I stopped using that paper years ago, but there were a few odd sheets and envelopes left in the old desk. We never fastened up the lid of the box before locking it in. The hand got out, found a pencil, wrote this note, and shoved it through the crack on to the floor, where Morton found it. That's plain as daylight.'

'But the hand couldn't write!'

'Couldn't it? You've not seen it do the things I've seen.'

And he told Saunders more of what had happened at Eastbourne.

'Well,' said Saunders, 'in that case we have at least an explanation of the legacy. It was the hand which wrote, unknown to your uncle, that letter to your solicitor bequeathing itself to you. Your uncle had no more to do with that request than I. In fact, it would seem that he had some idea of this automatic writing and feared it.'

'Then if it's not my uncle, what is it?'

'I suppose some people might say that a disembodied spirit

had got your uncle to educate and prepare a little body for it. Now it's got into that little body and is off on its own.'

'Well, what are we to do?'

'We'll keep our eyes open,' said Saunders, 'and try to catch it. If we can't do that, we shall have to wait till the bally clockwork runs down. After all, if it's flesh and blood, it can't live forever.'

For two days nothing happened. Then Saunders saw it sliding down the banister in the hall. He was taken unawares and lost a full second before he started in pursuit, only to find that the thing had escaped him. Three days later Eustace, writing alone in the library at night, saw it sitting on an open book at the other end of the room. The fingers crept over the page, as if it were reading; but before he had time to get up from his seat, it had taken the alarm, and was pulling itself up the curtains. Eustace watched it grimly, as it hung on to the cornice with three fingers and flicked thumb and forefinger at him in an expression of scornful derisio.

'I know what I'll do,' he said. 'If I only get it into the open I'll set the dogs on to it.'

He spoke to Saunders of the suggestion.

'It's a jolly good idea,' he said; 'only we won't wait till we find it out of doors. We'll get the dogs. There are the two terriers and the under-keeper's Irish mongrel, that's on to rats like a flash. Yom-spaniel has not got spirit enough for this sort of game.'

They brought the dogs into the house, and the keeper's Irish mongrel chewed up the slippers, and the terriers tripped up Morton as he waited at table; but all three were welcome. Even false security is better than no security at all.

For a fortnight nothing happened. Then the hand was caught not by the dogs, but by Mrs Merrit's grey parrot. The bird was in the habit of periodically removing the pins that kept its seed-

and water-tin in place, and of escaping through the holes in the side of the cage. When once at liberty, Peter would show no inclination to return, and would often be about the house for days. Now, after six consecutive weeks of captivity, Peter had again discovered a new way of unloosing his bolts and was, at large, exploring the tapestried forests of the curtains and singing songs in praise of liberty from cornice and picture rail.

'It's no use your trying to catch him,' said Eustace to Mrs Merrit, as she came into the study one afternoon towards dusk with a step-ladder. 'You'd much better leave Peter alone. Starve him into surrender, Mrs Merrit; and don't leave bananas and seed about for him to peck at when he fancies he's hungry. You're far too soft-hearted.'

'Well, sir, I see he's right out of reach now on that picture-rail; so if you wouldn't mind closing the door, sir, when you leave the room, I'll bring his cage in tonight and put some meat inside it. He's that fond of meat, though it does make him pull out his feathers to suck the quills. They *do* say that if you cook—'

'Never mind, Mrs Merrit,' said Eustace, who was busy writing; 'that will do; I'll keep an eye on the bird.'

For a short time there was silence in the room.

'Scratch poor Peter,' said the bird. 'Scratch poor old Peter!'

'Be quiet, you beastly bird!'

'Poor old Peter! Scratch poor Peter; do!'

'I'm more likely to wring your neck, if I get hold of you.' He looked up at the picture-rail, and there was the hand, holding on to a hook with three fingers, and slowly scratching the head of the parrot with the fourth. Eustace ran to the bell and pressed it hard; then across to the window, which he closed with a bang. Frightened by the noise, the parrot shook its wings preparatory to flight, and, as it did so, the fingers of the hand got hold of it by the throat. There was a shrill scream from Peter, as he fluttered across the room, wheeling round in circles that ever descended, borne down under the weight that clung to him. The bird dropped at last quite suddenly, and Eustace saw fingers and feathers rolled into an inextricable mass on the floor. The struggle abruptly ceased, as finger and thumb squeezed the neck; the bird's eyes rolled up to show the white, and there was a faint, half-choked gurgle. But, before the fingers had time to loose their hold, Eustace had them in his own.

'Send Mr Saunders here at once,' he said to the maid who came in answer to the bell. 'Tell him I want him immediately.'

Then he went with the hand to the fire. There was a ragged gash across the back, where the bird's beak had torn it, but no blood oozed from the wound. He noted with disgust that the nails had grown long and discoloured.

'I'll burn the beastly thing,' he said. But he could not burn it. He tried to throw it into the flames, but his own hands, as if impelled by some old primitive feeling, would not let him. And so Saunders found him, pale and irresolute, with the hand still clasped tightly in his fingers.

'I've got it at last,' he said, in a tone of triumph.

'Good, let's have a look at it.'

'Not when it's loose. Get me some nails and a hammer and a board of some sort.'

'Can you hold it all right?'

'Yes, the thing's quite limp; tired out with throttling poor old Peter, I should say.'

'And now,' said Saunders, when he returned with the things, 'what are we going to do?'

'Drive a nail through it first, so that it can't get away. Then we can take our time over examining it.'

'Do it yourself,' said Saunders. 'I don't mind helping you with guinea-pigs occasionally, when there's something to be learned, partly because I don't fear a guinea-pig's revenge. This thing's different.'

'Oh, my aunt!' he giggled hysterically, 'look at it now.' For the hand was writhing in agonized contortions, squirming and wriggling upon the nail like a worm upon the hook.

'Well,' said Saunders, 'you've done it now. I'll leave you to examine it.'

'Don't go, in heaven's name! Cover it up, man; cover it up! Shove a cloth over it! Here!' and he pulled off the antimacassar from the back of a chair and wrapped the board in it. 'Now get the keys from my pocket and open the safe. Chuck the other things out. Oh, Lord, it's getting itself into frightful knots! Open it quick!' He threw the thing in and banged the door.

'We'll keep it there till it dies,' he said. 'May I burn in hell, if I ever open the door of that safe again.'

Mrs Merrit departed at the end of the month. Her successor, Mrs Handyside, certainly was more successful in the management of the servants. Early in her rule she declared that she would stand no nonsense, and gossip soon withered and died.

'I shouldn't be surprised if Eustace married one of these days,' said Saunders. 'Well, I'm in no hurry for such an event. I know him far too well for the future Mrs Borlsover to like me. It will be the same old story again; a long friendship slowly made—marriage—and a long friendship quickly forgotten.'

But Eustace did not follow the advice of his uncle and marry. Old habits crept over and covered his new experience. He was, if anything, less morose, and showed a great inclination to take his natural part in country society.

Then came the burglary. The man, it was said, broke into the house by way of the conservatory. It was really little more than an attempt, for they only succeeded in carrying away a few pieces of plate from the pantry. The safe in the study was certainly found open and empty, but, as Mr Borlsover informed the police inspector, he had kept nothing of value in it during the last six months.

'Then you're lucky in getting off so easily, sir,' the man replied. 'By the way they have gone about their business I should say they were experienced cracksmen. They must have caught the alarm when they were just beginning their evening's work.'

'Yes,' said Eustace, 'I suppose I am lucky.'

'I've no doubt,' said the inspector, 'that we shall be able to trace the men. I've said that they must have been old hands at the game. The way they got in and opened the safe shows that. But there's one little thing that puzzles me. One of them was careless enough not to wear gloves, and I'm bothered if I know what he was trying to do. I've traced his finger-marks on the new varnish on the window-sashes in every one of the downstairs rooms. They are very distinctive ones too.'

'Right hand or left or both?' asked Eustace.

'Oh, right every time. That's the funny thing. He must have been a foolhardy fellow, and I rather think it was him that wrote that.' He took out a slip of paper from his pocket. 'That's what he wrote, sir: "I've got out, Eustace Borlsover, but I'll be back before long." Some jailbird just escaped, I suppose. It will make it all the easier for us to trace him. Do you know the writing, sir?'

'No,' said Eustace. 'It's not the writing of anyone I know.'

'I'm not going to stay here any longer,' said Eustace to Saunders at luncheon. 'I've got on far better during the last six months than I expected, but I'm not going to run the risk of seeing that thing again. I shall go up to town this afternoon. Get Morton to put my things together, and join me with the car at Brighton on the day after tomorrow. And bring the proofs of those two papers with you. We'll run over them together.'

'How long are you going to be away?'

'I can't say for certain, but be prepared to stay for some time. We've stuck to work pretty closely through the summer, and I for one need a holiday. I'll engage the rooms at Brighton. You'll find it best to break the journey at Hitchin. I'll wire to you there at the "Crown" to tell you the Brighton address.'

The house he chose at Brighton was in a terrace. He had been there before. It was kept by his old college gyp, a man of discreet silence, who was admirably partnered by an excellent cook. The rooms were on the first floor. The two bedrooms were at the back, and opened out of each other. 'Mr Saunders can have the smaller one, though it is the only one with a fire-place,' he said. 'I'll stick to the larger of the two, since it's got a bathroom adjoining. I wonder what time he'll arrive with the car.'

Saunders came about seven, cold and cross and dirty. 'We'll light the fire in the dining-room,' said Eustace, 'and get Prince to unpack some of the things while we are at dinner. What were the roads like?'

'Rotten. Swimming with mud, and a beastly cold wind against us all day. And this is July. Dear Old England!'

'Yes,' said Eustace, 'I think we might do worse than leave Old England for a few months.'

They turned in soon after twelve.

'You oughtn't to feel cold, Saunders,' said Eustace, 'when you can afford to sport a great fur-lined coat like this. 'You do yourself very well, all things considered. Look at those gloves, for instance. Who could possibly feel cold when wearing them?'

'They are far too clumsy, though, for driving. Try them on and see,' and he tossed them through the door on to Eustace's bed and went on with his unpacking. A minute later he heard a shrill cry of terror. 'Oh, Lord,' he heard, 'it's in the glove! Quick, Saunders quick!' Then came a smacking thud. Eustace had thrown it from him. 'I've chucked it into the bathroom,' he gasped; 'it's hit the wall and fallen into the bath. Come now, if you want to help,' Saunders, with a lighted candle in his hand, looked over the edge of the bath. There it was, old and maimed, dumb and blind, with a ragged hole in the middle, crawling, staggering, trying to creep up the slippery sides, only to fall back helpless.

'Stay there,' said Saunders. 'I'll empty a collar-box or something and we'll jam it in. It can't get out while I'm away.'

'Yes, it can,' shouted Eustace. 'It's getting out now; it's climbing up the plug-chain.—No, you brute, you filthy brute, you don't!—Come back, Saunders; it's getting away from me. I can't hold it; it's all slippery. Curse its claws! Shut the window, you idiot! It's got out!' There was the sound of something dropping on to the hard flag-stones below, and Eustace fell back fainting.

For a fortnight he was ill.

'I don't know what to make of it,' the doctor said to Saunders. 'I can only suppose that Mr Borlsover has suffered some great emotional shock. You had better let me send someone to help you nurse him. And by all means indulge that whim of his never to be left alone in the dark. I would keep a light burning all night, if I were you. But he *must* have more fresh air. It's perfectly absurd, this hatred of open windows.'

Eustace would have no one with him but Saunders. 'I don't want the other man,' he said. 'They'd smuggle it in somehow. I know they would.'

'Don't worry about it, old chap. This sort of thing can't go on indefinitely. You know I saw it this time as well as you. It wasn't half so active. It won't go on living much longer, especially after that fall. I heard it hit the flags myself. As soon as you're a bit stronger, we'll leave this place, not bag and baggage, but with only the clothes on our backs, so that it won't be able to hide anywhere. We'll escape it that way. We won't give any address, and we won't have any parcels sent after us. Cheer up, Eustace! You'll be well-enough to leave in a day or two. The doctor says I can take you out in a chair tomorrow.'

'What have I done?' asked Eustace. 'Why does it come after me? I'm no worse than other men. I'm no worse than you, Saunders; you know I'm not. It was you who was at the bottom of that dirty business in San Diego, and that was fifteen years ago.'

'It's not that, of course,' said Saunders. 'We are in the twentieth century, and even the parsons have dropped the idea of your old sins finding you out. Before you caught the hand in the library, it was filled with pure malevolence—to you and all mankind. After you spiked it through with that nail, it naturally forgot about other people and concentrated its attention on you. It was shut up in that safe, you know, for nearly six months. That gives plenty of time for thinking of revenge.'

Eustace Borlsover would not leave his room, but he thought there might be something in Saunders's suggestion of a sudden departure from Brighton. He began rapidly to regain his strength.

'We'll go on the first of September,' he said.

The evening of the thirty-first of August was oppressively warm. Though at midday the windows had been wide open, they had been shut an hour or so before dusk. Mrs Prince had long since ceased to wonder at the strange habits of the gentlemen on the first floor. Soon after their arrival she had been told to take down the heavy window curtains in the two bedrooms, and day by day the rooms had seemed to grow more bare. Nothing was left lying about.

'Mr Borlsover doesn't like to have any place where dirt can collect,' Saunders had said as an excuse. 'He likes to see into all the corners of the room.'

'Couldn't I open the window just a little?' he said to Eustace that evening. 'We're simply roasting in here, you know.'

'No, leave well alone. We're not a couple of boarding-school misses fresh from a course of hygiene lectures. Get the chess-board out.'

They sat down and played. At ten o'clock Mrs Prince came to the door with a note. 'I am sorry I didn't bring it before,' she said, 'but it was left in the letter-box.'

'Open it, Saunders, and see if it wants answering.'

It was very brief. There was neither address nor signature.

'Will eleven o'clock tonight be suitable for our last appointment?'

'Who is it from?' asked Borlsover.

'It was meant for me,' said Saunders. 'There's no answer, Mrs Prince,' and he put the paper into his pocket.

'A dunning letter from a tailor; I suppose he must have got wind of our leaving.'

It was a clever lie, and Eustace asked no more questions. They went on with their game.

On the landing outside Saunders could hear the grandfather's clock whispering the seconds, blurting out the quarter-hours.

'Check,' said Eustace. The clock struck eleven. At the same time there was a gentle knocking on the door; it seemed to come from the bottom panel.

'Who's there?' asked Eustace.

There was no answer.

'Mrs Prince, is that you?'

'She is up above,' said Saunders; 'I can hear her walking

about the room.'

'Then lock the door; bolt it too. Your move, Saunders.'

While Saunders sat with his eyes on the chess-board, Eustace walked over to the window and examined the fastenings. He did the same in Saunders's room, and the bathroom. There were no doors between the three rooms, or he would have shut and locked them too.

'Now, Saunders,' he said, 'don't stay all night over your move. I've had time to smoke one cigarette already. It's bad to keep an invalid waiting. There's only one possible thing for you to do. What was that?'

'The ivy blowing against the window. There, it's your move now, Eustace.'

'It wasn't the ivy, you idiot! It was someone tapping at the window,' and he pulled up the blind. On the outer side of the window, clinging to the sash, was the hand.

'What is it that it's holding?'

'It's a pocket-knife. It's going to try to open the window by pushing back the fastener with the blade.'

'Well, let it try,' said Eustace. 'Those fasteners screw down; they can't be opened that way. Anyhow, we'll close the shutters. It's your move, Saunders; I've played.'

But Saunders found it impossible to fix his attention on the game. He could not understand Eustace, who seemed all at once to have lost his fear. 'What do you say to some wine?' he asked. 'You seem to be taking things coolly, but I don't mind confessing that I'm in a blessed funk.'

'You've no need to be. There's nothing supernatural about that hand, Saunders. I mean it seems to be governed by the laws of time and space. It's not the sort of thing that vanishes into thin air or slides through oaken doors. And since that's so, I defy it to get in here. We'll leave the place in the morning. I for one have bottomed the depths of fear. Fill your glass, man! The windows are all shuttered; the door is locked and bolted. Pledge me my Uncle Adrian! Drink, man! What are you waiting for?'

Saunders was standing with his glass half raised. 'It can get in,' he said hoarsely; 'it can get in. We've forgotten. There's the fireplace in my bedroom. It will come down the chimney.'

'Quick!' said Eustace, as he rushed into the other room; 'we haven't a minute to lose. What can we do? Light the fire, Saunders. Give me a match, quick!'

'They must be all in the other room. I'll get them.'

'Hurry, man, for goodness' sake! Look in the bookcase! Look in the bathroom! Here, come and stand here; I'll look.'

'Be quick!' shouted Saunders. 'I can hear something!'

'Then plug a sheet from your bed up the chimney. No, here's a match!' He had found one at last that had slipped into a crack in the floor.

'Is the fire laid? Good, but it may not burn. I know—the oil from that old reading-lamp and this cotton-wool. Now the match, quick! Pull the sheet away, you fool! We don't want it now.'

There was a great roar from the grate, as the flames shot up. Saunders had been a fraction of a second too late with the sheet. The oil had fallen on to it. It, too, was burning.

'The whole place will be on fire!' cried Eustace, as he tried to beat out the flames with a blanket. 'It's no good! I can't manage it. You must open the door, Saunders, and get help.'

Saunders ran to the door and fumbled with the bolts. The key was stiff in the lock. 'Hurry,' shouted Eustace, 'or the heat will be too much for me.' The key turned in the lock at last. For half a second Saunders stopped to look back. Afterwards he could never be quite sure as to what he had seen, but at the time he thought that something black and charred was creeping slowly, very slowly, from the mass of flames towards Eustace Borlsover. For a moment he thought of returning to his friend; but the noise and the smell of the burning sent him running down the passage, crying: 'Fire! Fire!' He rushed to the telephone to summon help, and then back to the bathroom—he should have thought of that before—for water. As he burst into the bedroom there came a scream of terror which ended suddenly, and then the sound of a heavy fall.

This is the story which I heard on successive Saturday evenings from the senior mathematical master at a second-rate suburban school. For Saunders has had to earn a living in a way which other men might reckon less congenial than his old manner of life. I had mentioned by chance the name of Adrian Borlsover, and wondered at the time why he changed the conversation with such unusual abruptness. A week later Saunders began to tell me something of his own history; sordid enough, though shielded with a reserve I could well understand, for it had to cover not only his failings, but those of a dead friend. Of the final tragedy he was at first especially loath to speak; and it was only gradually that I was able to piece together the narrative of the preceding pages. Saunders was reluctant to draw any conclusions. At one time he thought that the fingered beast had been animated by the spirit of Sigismund Borlsover, a sinister eighteenth-century ancestor, who, according to legend, built and worshipped in the ugly pagan temple that overlooked the lake. At another time Saunders believed the spirit to belong to a man whom Eustace had once employed as a laboratory assistant, 'a black-haired, spiteful little brute,' he said, 'who died cursing his doctor, because the fellow couldn't help him to live to settle some paltry score with Borlsover.'

From the point of view of direct contemporary evidence, Saunders's story is practically uncorroborated. All the letters mentioned in the narrative were destroyed, with the exception of the last note which Eustace received, or rather which he would have received, had not Saunders intercepted it. That I have seen myself. The handwriting was thin and shaky, the handwriting of an old man. I remember the Greek V was used in 'appointment'. A little thing that amused me at the time was that Saunders seemed to keep the note pressed between the pages of his Bible.

I had seen Adrian Borlsover once. Saunders I learnt to know well. It was by chance, however, and not by design, that I met a third person of the story, Morton, the butler. Saunders and I were walking in the Zoological Gardens one Sunday afternoon, when he called my attention to an old man who was standing before the door of the Reptile House.

'Why, Morton,' he said, clapping him on the back, 'how is the world treating you?'

'Poorly, Mr Saunders,' said the old fellow, though his face lighted up at the greeting. 'The winters drag terribly nowadays. There don't seem no summers or springs.'

'You haven't found what you were looking for, I suppose?'

'No, sir, not yet; but I shall some day. I always told them that Mr Borlsover kept some queer animals.'

'And what is he looking for?' I asked, when we had parted from him.

'A beast with five fingers,' said Saunders. 'This afternoon, since he has been in the Reptile House, I suppose it will be a reptile with a hand. Next week it will be a monkey with practically no body. The poor old chap is a born materialist.'

THE JUDGE'S HOUSE

Bram Stoker

When the time for his examination drew near, Malcolm
Malcolmson made up his mind to go somewhere to read
by himself. He feared the attractions of the seaside, and also he
feared complete rural isolation, for of old he knew its charms,
and so he determined to find some unpretentious little town
where there would be nothing to distract him. He refrained from
asking suggestions from any of his friends, for he argued that
each would recommend some place of which he had knowledge,
and where he had already acquaintances. As Malcolmson wished
to avoid friends, he had no wish to encumber himself with the
attention of friends' friends, and so he determined to look out
for a place for himself. He packed a portmanteau with some
clothes and all the books he required, and then took ticket for
the first name on the local time-table which he did not know.

When at the end of three hours' journey he alighted at
Benchurch, he felt satisfied that he had so far obliterated his
tracks as to be sure of having a peaceful opportunity of pursuing
his studies. He went straight to the one in which the sleepy
little place contained and put up for the night. Benchurch was
a market-town, and once in three weeks was crowded to excess,

but for the remainder of the twenty-one days it was as attractive as a desert. Malcolmson looked around the day after his arrival to try to find quarters more isolated than even so quiet an inn as 'The Good Traveller' afforded. There was only one place which took his fancy, and it certainly satisfied his wildest ideas regarding quiet; in fact, quiet was not the proper word to apply to it—desolation was the only term conveying any suitable idea of its isolation. It was an old rambling, heavy-built house of the Jacobean style, with heavy gables and windows, unusually small, and set higher than was customary in such houses, and was surrounded with a high brick wall massively built. Indeed, on examination it looked more like a fortified house than an ordinary dwelling. But all these things pleased Malcolmson. 'Here,' he thought, 'is the very spot I have been looking for, and if I can only get opportunity of using it I shall be happy.' His joy was increased when he realized beyond doubt that it was not at present inhabited.

From the post-office he got the name of the agent, who was rarely surprised at the application to rent a part of the old house. Mr Carnford, the local lawyer and agent, was a genial old gentleman, and frankly confessed his delight at anyone being willing to live in the house.

'To tell you the truth,' said he, 'I should be only too happy, on behalf of the owners, to let anyone have the house rent free for a term of years if only to accustom the people here to see it inhabited. It has been so long empty that some kind of absurd prejudice has grown up about it, and this can be best put down by its occupation—if only,' he added with a sly glance at Malcolmson, 'by a scholar like yourself, who wants its quiet for a time.'

Malcolmson thought it needless to ask the agent about the 'absurd prejudice'; he knew he would get more information, if he should require it, on that subject from other quarters. He paid his three months' rent, got a receipt, and the name of an old woman who would probably undertake to 'do' for him, and came away with the keys in his pocket. He then went to the landlady of the inn, who was a cheerful and most kindly person, and asked her advice as to such stores and provisions as he would be likely to require. She threw up her hands in amazement when he told her where he was going to settle himself.

'Not in the Judge's House!' she said, and grew pale as she spoke. He explained the locality of the house, saying that he did not know its name. When he had finished she answered:

'Aye, sure enough—sure enough the very place! It is the Judge's House sure enough.' He asked her to tell him about the place, why so called, and what there was against it. She told him that it was so called locally because it had been many years before—how long she could not say, as she was herself from another part of the country, but she thought it must have been a hundred years or more—the abode of a judge who was held in great terror on account of his harsh sentences and hostility to prisoners at Assizes. As to what there was against the house itself, she could not tell. She had often asked, but no one could inform her; but there was a general feeling that there was *something*, and for her own part she would not take all the money in Drinkwarter's Bank and stay in the house an hour by herself. Then she apologized to Malcolmson for her disturbing talk.

'It is too bad of me, sir, and you—and a young gentleman, too—if you will pardon me saying it, going to live there all alone. If you were my boy—and you'll excuse me for saying it—you wouldn't sleep there a night, not if I had to go there myself and pull the big alarm bell that's on the roof!' The good creature was so manifestly in earnest, and was so kindly in her intentions, that Malcolmson, although amused, was touched. He told her kindly how much he appreciated her interest in him, and added:

'But, my dear Mrs Witham, indeed you need not be concerned about me! A man who is reading for the Mathematical Tripos has too much to think of to be disturbed by any of these mysterious "somethings", and his work is of too exact and prosaic a kind to allow of his having any corner in his mind for mysteries of any kind. Harmonical Progression, Permutations and Combinations, and Elliptic Functions have sufficient mysteries for me!'

Mrs Witham kindly undertook to see after his commissions, and he went himself to look for the old woman who had been recommended to him. When he returned to the Judge's House with her, after an interval of a couple of hours, he found Mrs Witham herself waiting with several men and boys carrying parcels, and an upholsterer's man with a bed in a cart, for she said, though tables and chairs might be all very well, a bed that hadn't been aired for maybe fifty years was not proper for young bones to lie on. She was evidently curious to see the inside of the house; and though manifestly so afraid of the 'somethings' that at the slightest sound she clutched on to Malcolmson, whom she never left for a moment, she went over the whole place.

After his examination of the house, Malcolmson decided to take up his abode in the great dining-room, which was big enough to serve for all his requirements; and Mrs Witham, with the aid of the charwoman, Mrs Dempster, proceeded to arrange matters. When the hampers were brought in and unpacked, Malcolmson saw that with much kind forethought she had sent from her own kitchen sufficient provisions to last for a few days.

Before going she expressed all sorts of kind wishes, and at the door turned and said:

'And perhaps, sir, as the room is big and draughty it might be well to have one of those big screens put round your bed at night—though, truth to tell, I would die myself if I were to be so shut in with all kinds of—of "things", that put their heads round the sides, or over the top, and look on me!' The image which she had called up was too much for her nerves, and she fled incontinently.

Mrs Dempster sniffed in a superior manner as the landlady disappeared and remarked that for her own part she wasn't afraid of all the bogies in the kingdom.

'I'll tell you what it is, sir,' she said, 'bogies is all kinds and sorts of things—except bogies! Rats and mice, and beetles; and creaky doors, and loose slates, and broken panes, and stiff drawer handles, that stay out when you pull them and then fall down in the middle of the night. Look at the wainscot of the room! It is old—hundreds of years old! Do you think there's no rats and beetles there! And do you imagine, sir, that you won't see none of them! Rats is bogies, I tell you and bogies is rats; and don't you get to think anything else!'

'Mrs Dempster,' said Malcolmson gravely, making her a polite bow, 'you know more than a Senior Wrangler! And let me say that as a mark of esteem for your indubitable soundness of head and heart, I shall, when I go, give you possession of this house, and let you stay here by yourself for the last two months of my tenancy, for four weeks will serve my purpose.'

'Thank you kindly, sir!' she answered, 'but I couldn't sleep away from home a night. I am in Greenhow's Charity, and if I slept a night away from my rooms I should lose all I have got to live on. The rules is very strict; and there's too many watching for a vacancy for me to run any risks in the matter. Only for that, sir, I'd gladly come here and attend on you altogether during your stay.'

'My good woman,' said Malcolmson hastily, 'I have come here on purpose to obtain solitude; and believe me that I am grateful to the late Greenhow for having so organized his admirable charity—whatever it is—that I am perforce denied the opportunity of suffering from such a form of temptation! Saint Anthony himself could not be more rigid on the point!'

The old woman laughed harshly. 'Ah, you young gentlemen,' she said, 'you don't fear for naught; and belike you'll get all the solitude you want here.' She set to work with her cleaning; and by nightfall, when Malcolmson returned from his walk—he always had one of his books to study as he walked—he found the room swept and tidied, a fire burning in the old hearth, the lamp lit, and the table spread for supper with Mrs Witham's excellent fare. 'This is comfort, indeed,' he said, as he rubbed his hands.

When he had finished his supper and lifted the tray to the other end of the great oak dining-table, he got out his books again, put fresh wood on the fire, trimmed his lamp, and set himself down to a spell of real hard work. He went on without pause till about eleven o'clock, when he knocked off for a bit to fix his fire and lamp and to make himself a cup of tea. He had always been a tea-drinker, and during his college life had sat late at work and had taken tea late. The rest was a great luxury to him, and he enjoyed it with a sense of delicious, voluptuous ease. The renewed fire leaped and sparkled and threw quaint shadows through the great old room; and as he sipped his hot tea, he revelled in the sense of isolation from his kind. Then it was that he began to notice for the first time what a noise the rats were making.

'Surely,' he thought, 'they cannot have been at it all the time I was reading. Had they been, I must have noticed it!' Presently, when the noise increased, he satisfied himself that it was really new. It was evident that at first the rats had been frightened at the presence of a stranger and the light of fire and lamp, but that as the time went on, they had grown bolder and were now disporting themselves as was their wont.

How busy they were! And hark to the strange noises! Up and down behind the old wainscot, over the ceiling and under the floor they raced, and gnawed, and scratched! Malcolmson smiled to himself as he recalled to mind the saying of Mrs Dempster, 'Bogies is rats, and rats is bogies!' The tea began to have its effect of intellectual and nervous stimulus; he saw with joy another long spell of work to be done before the night was past, and in the sense of security which it gave him, he allowed himself the luxury of a good look round the room. He took his lamp in one hand and went all around, wondering that so quaint and beautiful an old house had been so long neglected. The carving of the oak on the panels of the wainscot was fine, and on and round the doors and windows it was beautiful and of rare merit. There were some old pictures on the walls, but they were coated so thick with dust and dirt that he could not distinguish any detail of them, though he held his lamp as high as he could over his head. Here and there, as he went round, he saw some crack or hole blocked for a moment by the face of a rat with its bright eyes glittering in the light, but in an instant it was gone, and a squeak and a scamper followed.

The thing that most struck him, however, was the rope of the great alarm bell on the roof, which hung down in a corner of the room on the right-hand side of the fireplace. He pulled up close to the hearth a great high-backed carved oak chair, and sat down to his last cup of tea. When this was done, he made up the fire and went back to his work, sitting at the corner of the table, having the fire to his left. For a while the rats disturbed him somewhat with their perpetual scampering, but he got accustomed to the noise as one does to the ticking of a clock or to the roar of moving water; and he became so immersed in his work that everything in the world, except the problem which he was trying to solve, passed away from him.

He suddenly looked up; his problem was still unsolved, and there was in the air that sense of the hour before the dawn, which is a dread to doubtful life. The noise of the rats had ceased. Indeed it seemed to him that it must have ceased but lately, and that it was the sudden cessation which had disturbed him. The fire had fallen low, but still it threw out a deep red glow. As he looked he started in spite of his *sang froid*.

There on the great high-backed carved oak chair by the right side of the fireplace sat an enormous rat, steadily glaring at him with baleful eyes. He made a motion to it as though to hunt it away, but it did not stir. Then he made the motion of throwing something. Still it did not stir, but showed its great white teeth angrily, and its cruel eyes shone in the lamplight with an added vindictiveness.

Malcolmson felt amazed, and seizing the poker from the hearth ran at it to kill it. Before, however, he could strike it, the rat, with a squeak that sounded like the concentration of hate, jumped upon the floor, and running up the rope of the alarm bell disappeared in the darkness beyond the range of the green-shaded lamp. Instantly, strange to say, the noisy scampering of the rats in the wainscot began again.

By this time Malcolmson's mind was quite off the problem; and as a shrill cock-crow outside told him of the approach of morning, he went to bed to sleep.

He slept so sound that he was not even waked by Mrs Dempster coming in to make up his room. It was only when she had tidied up the place and got his breakfast ready, and tapped on the screen which closed in his bed, that he woke. He was a little tired still after his night's hard work, but a strong cup of tea soon freshened him up, and, taking his book, he went out for his morning walk, bringing with him a few sandwiches lest he should not care to return till dinner time. He found a quiet walk between high elms some way outside the town, and here he spent the greater part of the day studying his Laplace. On his return he looked in to see Mrs Witham and to thank her for her kindness. When she saw him coming through the diamond-paned bay-window of her sanctum, she came out to meet him and asked him in. She looked at him searchingly and shook her head as she said:

'You must not overdo it, sir. You are paler this morning than you should be. Too late hours and too hard work on the brain isn't good for any man! But tell me, sir, how did you pass the night? Well, I hope? But, my heart! sir, I was glad when Mrs Dempster told me this morning that you were all right and sleeping sound when she went in.'

'Oh, I was all right,' he answered, smiling, 'the "somethings" didn't worry me, as yet. Only the rats; and they had a circus, I tell you, all over the place. There was one wicked-looking old devil that sat up on my own chair by the fire, and wouldn't go till I took the poker to him, and then he ran up the rope of the alarm bell and got to somewhere up the wall or the ceiling—I couldn't see where, it was so dark.'

'Mercy on us,' said Mrs Witham, 'an old devil, and sitting on a chair by the fireside! Take care, sir! Take care! There's many a true word spoken in jest.'

'How do you mean? 'pon my word I don't understand.'

'An old devil! The old devil, perhaps. There! sir, you needn't laugh,' for Malcolmson had broken into a hearty peal. 'You young folks thinks it easy to laugh at things that makes older

ones shudder. Never mind, sir,! Never mind! Please God, you'll
laugh all the time. It's what I wish you myself!' and the good
lady beamed all over in sympathy with his enjoyment, her fears
gone for a moment.

'Oh, forgive me!' said Malcolmson presently. 'Don't think
me rude; but the idea was too much for me—that the old devil
himself was on the chair last night!' And at the thought he
laughed again. Then he went home to dinner.

This evening the scampering of the rats began earlier; indeed
it had been going on before his arrival, and only ceased whilst
his presence by its freshness disturbed them. After dinner he
sat by the fire for a while and had a smoke; and then, having
cleared his table, began to work as before. Tonight the rats
disturbed him more than they had done on the previous night.
How they scampered up and down and under and over! How
they squeaked, and scratched, and gnawed! How they, getting
bolder by degrees, came to the mouths of their holes and to
the chinks and cracks and crannies in the wainscoting till their
eyes shone like tiny lamps as the firelight rose and fell. But
to him, now doubtless accustomed to them, their eyes were
not wicked; only their playfulness touched him. Sometimes the
boldest of them made sallies out on the floor or along the
mouldings of the wainscot. Now and again as they disturbed
him, Malcolmson made a sound to frighten them, smiting the
table with his hand or giving a fierce 'Hsh, hsh,' so that they
fled straightway to their holes.

And so the early part of the night wore on; and despite the
noise, Malcolmson got more and more immersed in his work.

All at once he stopped, as on the previous night, being
overcome by a sudden sense of silence. There was not the
faintest sound of gnaw, or scratch, or squeak. The silence was
as of the grave. He remembered the odd occurrence of the

previous night, and instinctively he looked at the chair standing close by the fireside. And then a very odd sensation thrilled through him.

There, on the great old high-backed carved oak chair beside the fireplace sat the same enormous rat, steadily glaring at him with baleful eyes.

Instinctively he took the nearest thing to his hand, a book of logarithms, and flung it at it. The book was badly aimed and the rat did not stir, so again the poker performance of the previous night was repeated; and again the rat, being closely pursued, fled up the rope of the alarm bell. Strangely too, the departure of this rat was instantly followed by the renewal of the noise made by the general rat community. On this occasion, as on the previous one, Malcolmson could not see at what part of the room the rat disappeared, for the green shade of his lamp left the upper part of the room in darkness, and the fire had burned low.

On looking at his watch he found it was close to midnight; and, not sorry for the *divertissement*, he made up his fire and made himself his nightly pot of tea. He had got through a good spell of work, and thought himself entitled to a cigarette; and so he sat on the great carved oak chair before the fire and enjoyed it. Whilst smoking he began to think that he would like to know where the rat disappeared to, for he had certain ideas of the morrow not entirely disconnected with a rat-trap. Accordingly, he lit another lamp and placed it so that it would shine well into the right-hand corner of the wall by the fireplace. Then he got all the books he had with him, and placed them handy to throw at the vermin. Finally he lifted the rope of the alarm bell and placed the end of it on the table, fixing the extreme end under the lamp. As he handled it he could not help noticing how pliable it was, especially for so strong a rope, and one not in use. 'You could hang a man with it,' he thought to himself. When his preparations were made he looked around, and said complacently:

'There now, my friend, I think we shall learn something of you this time!' He began his work again, and though as before somewhat disturbed at first by the noise of the rats, soon lost himself in his propositions and problems.

Again, he was called to his immediate surroundings suddenly. This time it might not have been the sudden silence only which took his attention; there was a slight movement of the rope, and the lamp moved. Without stirring, he looked to see if his pile of books was within range, and then cast his eye along the rope. As he looked he saw the great rat drop from the rope on the oak armchair and sit there glaring at him. He raised a book in his right hand, and taking careful aim, flung it at the rat. The latter, with a quick movement, sprang aside and dodged the missile. He then took another book, and a third, and flung them one after another at the rat, but each time unsuccessfully. At last, as he stood with a book poised in his hand to throw, the rat squeaked and seemed afraid. This made Malcolmson more than ever eager to strike, and the book flew and struck the rat a resounding blow. It gave a terrified squeak, and turning on its pursuer a look of terrible malevolence, ran up the chair-back and made a great jump to the rope of the alarm bell and ran up it like lightning. The lamp rocked under the sudden strain, but it was a heavy one and did not topple over. Malcolmson kept his eyes on the rat and saw it by the light of the second lamp leap to a moulding of the wainscot and disappear through a hole in one of the great pictures which hung on the wall, obscured and invisible through its coating of dirt and dust.

'I shall look up my friends' habitation in the morning,' said the student, as he went over to collect his books. 'The third picture from the fireplace; I shall not forget.' He picked up the books one by one, commenting on them as he lifted them. '*Conic Sections* he does not mind, nor *Cycloidal Oscillations*, nor the *Principia*, nor *Quaternions*, nor *Thermodynamics*. Now for the book that fetched him!' Malcolmson took it up and looked at it. As he did so he started, and a sudden pallor overspread his face. He looked round uneasily and shivered slightly, as he murmured to himself:

'The Bible my mother gave me! What an odd coincidence.' He sat down to work again, and the rats in the wainscot renewed their gambols. They did not disturb him, however; somehow their presence gave him a sense of companionship. But he could not attend to his work, and after striving to master the subject on which he was engaged, he gave it up in despair, and went to bed as the first streak of dawn stole in through the eastern window.

He slept heavily but uneasily, and dreamed much; and when Mrs Dempster woke him late in the morning, he seemed ill at ease, and for a few minutes did not seem to realize exactly where he was. His first request rather surprised the servant.

'Mrs Dempster, when I am out today I wish you would get the steps and dust or wash those pictures—especially that one the third from the fireplace—I want to see what they are.'

Late in the afternoon Malcolmson worked at his books in the shaded walk, and the cheerfulness of the previous day came back to him as the day wore on, and he found that his reading was progressing well. He had worked out to a satisfactory conclusion all the problems which had as yet baffled him, and it was in a state of jubilation that he paid a visit to Mrs Witham at 'The Good Traveller'. He found a stranger in the cosy sitting-room with the landlady, who was introduced to him as Dr Thornhill. She was not quite at ease, and this, combined with the Doctor's plunging at once into a series of questions, made Malcolmson come to the conclusion that his presence was not an accident, so without preliminary he said:

'Dr Thornhill, I shall with pleasure answer you any question you may choose to ask me if you will answer me one question first.'

The doctor seemed surprised, but he smiled and answered at once. 'Done! What is it?'

'Did Mrs Witham ask you to come here and see me and advise me?'

Dr Thornhill for a moment was taken aback, and Mrs Witham got fiery red and turned away; but the doctor was a frank and ready man, and he answered at once and openly:

'She did, but she didn't intend you to know it. I suppose it was my clumsy haste that made you suspect. She told me that she did not like the idea of your being in that house all by yourself, and that she thought you took too much strong tea. In fact, she wants me to advise you if possible to give up the tea and the very late hours. I was a keen student in my time, so I suppose I may take the liberty of a college man, and without offence, advise you not quite as a stranger.'

Malcolmson with a bright smile held out his hand. 'Shake! as they say in America,' he said. 'I must thank you for your kindness and Mrs Witham too, and your kindness deserves a return on my part. I promise to take no more strong tea—no tea at all till you let me—and I shall go to bed tonight at one o'clock at the latest. Will that do?'

'Capital,' said the Doctor. 'Now tell us all that you noticed in the old house.' And so Malcolmson then and there told in minute detail all that had happened in the last two nights. He was interrupted every now and then by some exclamation from Mrs Witham, till finally when he told of the episode of the Bible, the landlady's pent-up emotions found vent in a shriek; and it was not till a stiff glass of brandy and water had been administered that she grew composed again. Dr Thornhill listened with a face of growing gravity, and when the narrative was complete and Mrs Witham had been restored, he asked:

'The rat always went up the rope of the alarm bell?'

'Always.'

'I suppose you know,' said the doctor after a pause, 'what the rope is?'

'No!'

'It is,' said the doctor slowly, 'the very rope which the hangman used for all the victims of the Judge's judicial rancour!' Here he was interrupted by another scream from Mrs Witham, and steps had to be taken for her recovery. Malcolmson, having looked at his watch and found that it was close to his dinner hour, had gone home before her complete recovery.

When Mrs Witham was herself again she almost assailed the doctor with angry questions as to what he meant by putting such horrible ideas into the poor young man's mind. 'He has quite enough there already to upset him,' she added. Dr Thornhill replied:

'My dear madam, I had a distinct purpose in it! I wanted to draw his attention to the hell rope, and to fix it there. It may be that he is in a highly overwrought state, and has been studying too much, although I am bound to say that he seems as sound and healthy a young man, mentally and bodily, as ever I saw—but then the rats—and that suggestion of the devil.' The doctor shook his head and went on. 'I would have offered to go and stay the first night with him but that I felt sure it would have been a cause of offence. He may get in the night some strange fright or hallucination; and if he does, I want him to pull that rope. All alone as he is, it will give us warning, and we may reach him in time to be of service. I shall be sitting up pretty late tonight and shall keep my ears open. Do not be alarmed if Benchurch gets a surprise before morning.'

'Oh, doctor, what do you mean? What do you mean?'

'I mean this; that possibly—nay, more probably—we shall hear the great alarm bell from the Judge's House tonight,' and the doctor made about as effective an exit as could be thought of.

When Malcolmson arrived home he found that it was a little after his usual time, and Mrs Dempster had gone away—the rule of Greenhow's Charity were not to be neglected. He was glad to see that the place was bright and tidy with a cheerful fire and a well-trimmed lamp. The evening was colder than might have been expected in April, and a heavy wind was blowing with such rapidly increasing strength that there was every promise of a storm during the night. For a few minutes after his entrance, the noise of the rats ceased; but so soon as they became accustomed to his presence they began again. He was glad to hear them, for he felt once more the feeling of companionship in their noise, and his mind ran back to the strange fact that they only ceased to manifest themselves when that other—the great rat with the baleful eyes—came upon the scene. The reading-lamp only was lit, and its green shade kept the ceiling and the upper part of the room in darkness, so that the cheerful light from the hearth spreading over the floor and shining on the white cloth laid over the end of the table was warm and cheery, Malcolmson sat down to his dinner with a good appetite and a buoyant spirit. After his dinner and a cigarette, he sat steadily down to work, determined not to let anything disturb him, for he remembered his promise to the doctor, and made up his mind to make the best of the time at his disposal.

For an hour or so he worked all right, and then his thoughts began to wander from his books. The actual circumstances around him, the calls on his physical attention, and his nervous susceptibility were not to be denied. By this time the wind had become a gale, and the gale a storm. The old house, solid though it was, seemed to shake to its foundations, and the storm roared and raged through its many chimneys and its queer old gables, producing strange, unearthly sounds in the empty rooms and corridors. Even the great alarm bell on the roof must have felt the force of the wind, for the rope rose and fell slightly, as though the bells were moved a little from time to time, and the limber rope fell on the oak floor with a hard and hollow sound.

As Malcolmson listened to it, he bethought himself of the doctor's words, 'It is the rope which the hangman used for the victims of the Judge's judicial rancour,' and he went over to the corner of the fireplace and took it in his hand to look at it. There seemed a sort of deadly interest in it, and as he stood there he lost himself for a moment in speculation as to who these victims were, and the grim wish of the Judge to have such a ghastly relic ever under his eyes. As he stood there, the swaying of the bell on the roof still lifted the rope now and again; but presently there came a new sensation—a sort of tremor in the rope, as though something was moving along it.

Looking up instinctively, Malcolmson saw the great rat coming slowly down towards him, glaring at him steadily. He dropped the rope and started back with a muttered curse, and the rat turning ran up the rope again and disappeared, and at the same instant Malcolmson became conscious that the noise of the rats, which had ceased for a while, began again.

All this set him thinking, and it occurred to him that he had not investigated the lair of the rat or looked at the pictures, as he had intended. He lit the other lamp without the shade, and, holding it up, went and stood opposite the third picture from the fireplace on the right-hand side where he had seen the rat disappear on the previous night.

At the first glance he started back so suddenly that he almost dropped the lamp, and a deadly pallor overspread his face. His knees shook, and heavy drops of sweat came on his forehead, and he trembled like an aspen. But he was young and plucky, and pulled himself together, and after the pause of a few seconds stepped forward again, raised the lamp, and examined the picture which had been dusted and washed, and now stood out clearly.

It was of a judge dressed in his robes of scarlet and ermine. His face was strong and merciless, evil, crafty, and vindictive, with a sensual mouth, hooked nose of ruddy colour, and shaped like the beak of a bird of prey. The rest of the face was of a cadaverous colour. The eyes were of peculiar brilliance and with a terribly malignant expression. As he looked at them, Malcolmson grew cold, for he saw there the very counterpart of the eyes of the great rat. The lamp almost fell from his hand as he saw the rat with its baleful eyes peering out through the hole in the corner of the picture, and noted the sudden cessation of the noise of the other rats. However, he pulled himself together, and went on with his examination of the picture.

The Judge was seated in a great high-backed carved oak chair, on the right-hand side of a great stone fireplace where, in the corner, a rope hung down from the ceiling, its end lying coiled on the floor. With a feeling of something like horror, Malcolmson recognized the scene of the room as it stood, and gazed around him in an awestruck manner, as though he expected to find some strange presence behind him. Then he looked over to the corner of the fireplace—and with a loud cry he let the lamp fall from his hand.

There, in the Judge's arm-chair, with the rope hanging behind, sat the rat with the Judge's baleful eyes, now intensified and with a fiendish leer. Save for the howling of the storm without, there was silence.

The fallen lamp recalled Malcolmson to himself. Fortunately it was of metal, and so the oil was not spilt. However, the practical need of attending to it settled at once his nervous apprehensions. When he had turned it out, he wiped his brow and thought for a moment.

'This will not do,' he said to himself. 'If I go on like this I shall become a crazy fool. This must stop! I promised the doctor I would not take tea. Faith, he was pretty right! My nerves must have been getting into a queer state. Funny I did not notice it. I never felt better in my life. However, it is all right now, and I shall not be such a fool again.'

Then he mixed himself a good stiff glass of brandy and water and resolutely sat down to his work.

It was nearly an hour when he looked up from his book, disturbed by the sudden stillness. Without, the wind howled and roared louder than ever, and the rain drove in sheets against the windows, beating like hail on the glass; but within there was no sound whatever, save the echo of the wind as it roared in the great chimney, and now and then a hiss as a few raindrops found their way down the chimney in a lull of the storm. The fire had fallen low and had ceased to flame, though it threw out a red glow. Malcolmson listened attentively, and presently heard a thin, squeaking noise, very faint. It came from the corner of the room where the rope hung down, and he thought it was the creaking of the rope on the floor as the swaying of the bell raised and lowered it. Looking up, however, he saw in the dim light the great rat clinging to the rope and gnawing it. The rope was already nearly gnawed through—he could see the lighter colour where the strands were laid bare. As he looked, the job was completed, and the severed end of the rope fell clattering on the oaken floor, whilst for an instant the great rat remained like a knob or tassel at the end of the rope, which now began to sway to and fro. Malcolmson felt for a moment another pang of terror as he thought that now the possibility of calling the outer world to his assistance was cut off, but an intense anger took its place, and seizing the book he was reading he hurled it at the rat. The blow was well-aimed, but before the missile could reach it, the rat dropped off and struck the floor with a soft thud. Malcolmson instantly rushed over towards it, but it darted away and disappeared in the darkness of the shadows of the room. Malcolmson felt that his work was over for the night, and determined then and there to vary the monotony of the proceedings by a hunt for the rat, and took off the green shade of the lamp so as to insure a wider spreading light. As he did so, the gloom of the upper part of the room was relieved, and in the new flood of light, great by comparison with the previous darkness, the pictures on the wall stood out boldly. From where he stood, Malcolmson saw right opposite to him the third picture on the wall from the right of the fireplace. He rubbed his eyes in surprise, and then a great fear began to come upon him.

In the centre of the picture was a great irregular patch of brown canvas, as fresh as when it was stretched on the frame. The background was as before, with chair and chimney-corner and rope, but the figure of the Judge had disappeared.

Malcolmson, almost in a chill of horror, turned slowly round and then he began to shake and tremble like a man in a palsy. His strength seemed to have left him, and he was incapable of action or movement, hardly even of thought. He could only see and hear.

There, on the great high-backed carved oak chair sat the Judge in his robes of scarlet and ermine, with his baleful eyes glaring vindictively, and a smile of triumph on the resolute, cruel mouth, as he lifted with his hands a black cap. Malcolmson felt as if the blood was running from his heart, as one does in moments of prolonged suspense. There was a singing in his ears. Without, he could hear the roar and howl of the tempest, and through it, swept on the storm, came the striking of midnight by the great chimes in the marketplace. He stood for a space of time that seemed to him endless, still as a statue and with wide-open, horror-struck eyes, breathless. As the clock struck, so the smile of triumph on the Judge's face intensified, and at the last stroke of midnight, he placed the black cap on his head.

Slowly and deliberately the Judge rose from his chair and picked up the piece of the rope of the alarm bell which lay on the floor, drew it through his hands, as if he enjoyed its touch, and then deliberately began to knot one end of it, fashioning it into a noose. This he tightened and tested with his foot, pulling hard at it till he was satisfied, and then making a running noose of it, which he held in his hand. Then he began to move along the table on the opposite side to Malcolmson, keeping his eyes on him until he had passed him, when with a quick movement he stood in front of the door. Malcolmson then began to feel that he was trapped and tried to think of what he should do. There was some fascination in the Judge's eyes, which he never took off him, and he had, perforce, to look. He saw the Judge approach—still keeping between him and the door—and raise the noose and throw it towards him as it to entangle him. With a great effort he made a quick movement to one side, and saw the rope fall beside him, and heard it strike the oaken floor. Again the Judge raised the noose and tried to ensnare him, ever keeping his baleful eyes fixed on him, and each time by a mighty effort the student just managed to evade it. So this went on for many times, the Judge seeming never discouraged nor discomposed at failure, but playing as a cat does with a mouse. At last in despair, which had reached its climax, Malcolmson cast a quick glance round him. The lamp seemed to have blazed up, and there was a fairly good light in the room. At the many rat-holes and in the chinks and crannies of the wainscot he saw the rats' eyes; and this aspect, that was purely physical, gave him a gleam of comfort. He looked around and saw that the rope of the great alarm bell was laden with rats. Every inch of it was covered with them, and more and more were pouring through the small circular hole in the ceiling whence it emerged, so that with their weight the bell was beginning to sway.

Hark! it had swayed till the clapper had touched the bell. The sound was but a tiny one but the bell was only beginning to sway, and it would increase.

At the sound, the Judge, who had been keeping his eyes fixed on Malcolmson, looked up, and a scowl of diabolical anger overspread his face. His eyes fairly glowed like hot coals, and he stamped his foot with a sound that seemed to make the house shake. A dreadful peal of thunder broke overhead as he raised the rope again, whilst the rats kept running up and down the rope as though working against time. This time, instead of throwing it, he drew close to his victim, and held open the noose as he approached. As he came closer, there seemed something paralysing in his very presence, and Malcolmson stood rigid as a corpse. He felt the Judge's icy fingers touch his throat as he adjusted the rope. The noose tightened—tightened. Then the Judge, taking the rigid form of the student in his arms, carried him over and placed him standing in the oak chair, and stepping up beside him, put his hand up and caught the end of the swaying rope of the alarm bell. As he raised his hand, the rats fled squeaking and disappeared through the hole in the ceiling. Taking the end of the noose which was round Malcolmson's neck, he tied it to the hanging bell-rope, and then descending pulled away the chair.

When the alarm bell of the Judge's House began to sound, a crowd soon assembled. Lights and torches of various kinds appeared, and soon a silent crowd was hurrying to the spot. They knocked loudly at the door, but there was no reply. Then they burst in the door and poured into the great dining-room, the doctor at the head.

There at the end of the rope of the great alarm bell hung the body of the student, and on the face of the Judge in the picture was a malignant smile.

THE STATEMENT OF RANDOLPH CARTER

H.P. Lovecraft

I repeat to you, gentlemen, that your inquisition is fruitless. Detain me here forever if you will; confine or execute me if you must have a victim to propitiate the illusion you call justice; but I can say no more than I have said already. Everything that I can remember, I have told you with perfect candour. Nothing has been distorted or concealed, and if anything remains vague, it is only because of the dark cloud which has come over my mind—that cloud and the nebulous nature of the horrors which brought it upon me.

Again I say, I do not know what has become of Harley Warren, though I think—almost hope—that he is in peaceful oblivion, if there be anywhere so blessed a thing. It is true that I have for five years been his closest friend, and a partial sharer of his terrible researches into the unknown. I will not deny, though my memory is uncertain and indistinct, that this witness of yours may have seen us together as he says, on the Gainsville pike, walking toward Big Cypress Swamp, at half past eleven on that awful night. That we bore electric lanterns, spades, and a curious coil of wire with attached instruments, I will even affirm; for these things all played a part in the single hideous scene which remains burned into my shaken recollection. But of what followed, and of the reason I was found alone and dazed on the edge of the swamp next morning, I must insist that I know nothing save what I have told you over and over again. You say to me that there is nothing in the swamp or near it which could form the setting of that frightful episode. I reply that I knew nothing beyond what I saw. Vision or nightmare it may have been—vision or nightmare I fervently hope it was— yet it is all that my mind retains of what took place in those shocking hours after we left the sight of men. And why Harley Warren did not return, he or his shade—or some nameless thing I cannot describe—alone can tell.

As I have said before, the weird studies of Harley Warren were well known to me, and to some extent shared by me. Of his vast collection of strange, rare books on forbidden subjects I have read all that are written in the languages of which I am master; but these are few as compared with those in languages I cannot understand. Most, I believe, are in Arabic; and the fiend-inspired book which brought on the end—the book which he carried in his pocket out of the world—was written in characters whose like I never saw elsewhere. Warren would never tell me just what was in that book. As to the nature of our studies— must I say again that I no longer retain full comprehension? It seems to me rather merciful that I do not, for they were terrible studies, which I pursued more through reluctant fascination than through actual inclination. Warren always dominated me, and sometimes I feared him. I remember how I shuddered at his facial expression on the night before the awful happening, when he talked so incessantly of his theory, why certain corpses never decay, but rest firm and fat in their tombs for a thousand years.

But I do not fear him now, for I suspect that he has known horrors beyond my ken. Now I fear for him.

Once more I say that I have no clear idea of our object on that night. Certainly, it had much to do with something in the book which Warren carried with him—that ancient book in undecipherable characters which had come to him from India a month before—but I swear I do not know what it was that we expected to find. Your witness says he saw us at half past eleven on the Gainsville pike, headed for Big Cypress Swamp. This is probably true, but I have no distinct memory of it. The picture seared into my soul is of one scene only, and the hour must have been long after midnight; for a waning crescent moon was high in the vaporous heavens.

The place was an ancient cemetery; so ancient that I trembled at the manifold signs of immemorial years. It was in a deep, damp hollow, overgrown with rank grass, moss, and curious creeping weeds, and filled with a vague stench which my idle fancy associated absurdly with rotting stone. On every hand were the signs of neglect and decrepitude, and I seemed haunted by the notion that Warren and I were the first living creatures to invade a lethal silence of centuries. Over the valley's rim, a wan, waning crescent moon peered through the noisome vapours that seemed to emanate from unheard of catacombs, and by its feeble, wavering beams I could distinguish a repellent array of antique slabs, urns, cenotaphs, and mausoleum facades; all crumbling, moss-grown, and moisture-stained, and partly concealed by the gross luxuriance of the unhealthy vegetation.

My first vivid impression of my own presence in this terrible necropolis concerns the act of pausing with Warren before a certain half-obliterated sepulchre and of throwing down some burdens which we seemed to have been carrying. I now observed that I had with me an electric lantern and two spades, whilst my companion was supplied with a similar lantern and a portable telephone outfit. No word was uttered, for the spot and the task seemed known to us; and without delay we seized our spades and commenced to clear away the grass, weeds, and drifted earth from the flat, archaic mortuary. After uncovering the entire surface, which consisted of three immense granite slabs, we stepped back some distance to survey the charnel scene; and Warren appeared to make some mental calculations. Then he returned to the sepulchre, and using his spade as a lever, sought to pry up the slab lying nearest to a stony ruin which may have been a monument in its day. He did not succeed, and motioned to me to come to his assistance. Finally our combined strength loosened the stone, which we raised and tipped to one side.

The removal of the slab revealed a black aperture, from which rushed an effluence of miasmal gases so nauseous that we started back in horror. After an interval, however, we approached the pit again, and found the exhalations less unbearable. Our lanterns disclosed the top of a flight of stone steps, dripping with some detestable ichor of the inner earth, and bordered by moist walls encrusted with niter. And now for the first time my memory records verbal discourse—Warren addressing me at length in his mellow tenor voice; a voice singularly unperturbed by our awesome surroundings.

'I'm sorry to have to ask you to stay on the surface,' he said, 'but it would be a crime to let anyone with your frail nerves go down there. You can't imagine, even from what you have read and from what I've told you, the things I shall have to see and do. It's fiendish work. Carter, and I doubt if any man without ironclad sensibilities could ever see it through and come up alive and sane. I don't wish to offend you, and Heaven knows I'd be glad enough to have you with me; but the responsibility is in a certain sense mine, and I couldn't drag a bundle of nerves like you down to probable death or madness. I tell you, you can't imagine what the thing is really like! But I promise to keep you informed over the telephone of every move—you see I've enough wire here to reach to the center of the earth and back!'

I can still hear, in memory, those coolly spoken words; and I can still remember my remonstrances. I seemed desperately anxious to accompany my friend into those sepulchral depths, yet he proved inflexibly obdurate. At one time he threatened to abandon the expedition if I remained insistent; a threat which proved effective, since he alone held the key to the thing. All this I can still remember, though I no longer know what manner of thing we sought. After he had obtained my reluctant acquiescence in his design, Warren picked up the reel of wire and adjusted the instruments. At his nod I took one of the latter and seated myself upon an aged, discolored gravestone close by the newly uncovered aperture. Then he shook my hand, shouldered the coil of wire, and disappeared within that indescribable ossuary.

For a minute I kept sight of the glow of his lantern, and heard the rustle of the wire as he laid it down after him; but the glow soon disappeared abruptly, as if a turn in the stone staircase had been encountered, and the sound died away almost as quickly. I was alone, yet bound to the unknown depths by those magic strands whose insulated surface lay green beneath the struggling beams of that waning crescent moon.

I constantly consulted my watch by the light of my electric lantern, and listened with feverish anxiety at the receiver of the telephone; but for more than a quarter of an hour heard nothing. Then a faint clicking came from the instrument, and I called down to my friend in a tense voice. Apprehensive as I was, I was nevertheless unprepared for the words which came up from that uncanny vault in accents more alarmed and quivering than any I had heard before from Harley Warren. He who had so calmly left me a little while previously, now called from below in a shaky whisper more portentous than the loudest shriek;

'God! If you could see what I am seeing!'

I could not answer. Speechless, I could only wait. Then came the frenzied tones again:

'Carter, it's terrible—monstrous—unbelievable!'

This time my voice did not fail me, and I poured into the transmitter a flood of excited questions. Terrified, I continued to repeat, 'Warren, what is it? What is it?'

Once more came the voice of my friend, still hoarse with fear, and now apparently tinged with despair:

'I can't tell you, Carter! It's too utterly beyond thought—I dare not tell you—no man could know it and live—Great God! I never dreamed of this!'

Stillness again, save for my now incoherent torrent of shuddering inquiry. Then the voice of Warren in a pitch of wilder consternation:

'Carter! for the love of God, put back the slab and get out of this if you can! Quick!—leave everything else and make for the outside—it's your only chance! Do as I say, and don't ask me to explain!'

I heard, yet was able only to repeat my frantic questions. Around me were the tombs and the darkness and the shadows; below me, some peril beyond the radius of the human imagination. But my friend was in greater danger than I, and through my fear I felt a vague resentment that he should deem me capable of deserting him under such circumstances. More clicking, and after a pause a piteous cry from Warren:

'Beat it! For God's sake, put back the slab and beat it, Carter!'

Something in the boyish slang of my evidently stricken companion unleashed my faculties. I formed and shouted a resolution, 'Warren, brace up! I'm coming down!' But at this offer the tone of my auditor changed to a scream of utter despair:

'Don't! You can't understand! It's too late—and my own fault. Put back the slab and run—there's nothing else you or anyone can do now!'

The tone changed again, this time acquiring a softer quality, as of hopeless resignation. Yet it remained tense through anxiety for me.

'Quick—before it's too late!'

I tried not to heed him; tried to break through the paralysis which held me, and to fulfil my vow to rush down to his aid. But his next whisper found me still held inert in the chains of stark horror.

'Carter—hurry! It's no use—you must go—better one than two—the slab—'

A pause, more clicking, then the faint voice of Warren:

'Nearly over now—don't make it harder—cover up those damned steps and run for your life—you're losing time—so long, Carter—won't see you again.'

Here Warren's whisper swelled into a cry; a cry that gradually rose to a shriek fraught with all the horror of the ages—

'Curse these hellish things—legions—My God! Beat it! Beat it! BEAT IT!'

After that was silence. I know not how many interminable cons I sat stupefied; whispering, muttering, calling, screaming into that telephone. Over and over again through those eons I whispered and muttered, called, shouted, and screamed, 'Warren! Warren! Answer me—are you there?'

And then there came to me the crowning horror of all— the unbelievable, unthinkable, almost unmentionable thing. I have said that eons seemed to elapse after Warren shrieked forth his last despairing warning, and that only my own cries now broke the hideous silence. But after a while there was a further clicking in the receiver, and I strained my ears to listen. Again I called down, 'Warren, are you there?' and in answer heard the thing which has brought this cloud over my mind. I do not try, gentlemen, to account for that thing—that voice— nor can I venture to describe it in detail, since the first words took away my consciousness and created a mental blank which reaches to the time of my awakening in the hospital. Shall I say that the voice was deep; hollow; gelatinous; remote; unearthly; inhuman; disembodied? What shall I say? It was the end of my experience, and is the end of my story. I heard it, and knew no more—heard it as I sat petrified in that unknown cemetery in the hollow, amidst the crumbling stones and the falling tombs, the rank vegetation and the miasmal vapours—heard it well up from the innermost depths of that damnable open sepulchre as I watched amorphous, necrophagous shadows dance beneath an accursed waning moon.

And this is what it said:

'You fool, Warren is DEAD!'

WHEN AL CAPONE WAS AMBUSHED

Jack Bilbo

When he was twenty, Jack Bilbo was robbed by an American gangster on Broadway. A week or so later, down and out, he meets this same gangster again who gives him food and offers him work with 'the gangs'. Not until this German boy has been working with them for some time does he learn that he is part of Al Capone's giant organization. His story opens now, when O'Connor, one of Al Capone's lieutenants, got him enrolled as the Boss's personal bodyguard.

At eleven-thirty O'Connor came to the house, and called me. 'I have told the Boss about you,' he said. 'You are to start work as his bodyguard on trial. I hope that all will go well.'

We started off with Conny—eight of us—in two cars. On the way Conny explained my new job to me.

'The bodyguard is responsible for the safety of the Boss,' he said. 'Your job is based on the assumption that his life is always being threatened, usually by enemy gangs but sometimes by the police. We gangsters can't even trust the police these days. There are thirty-six men in the bodyguard team and eighteen of them are on duty each week. Six men, with a leader, are always on duty at his home or in his office; the watch changes every eight hours. In your spare time you can do outside "jobs" if you want to, but nothing that will bring you in danger.' He paused, then continued, emphasizing every word, 'Remember— no stranger is allowed closer to the Boss than five paces. If any one acts suspiciously, shoot him first and ask questions later.'

Conny introduced me to the man sitting next to me, a swarthy individual called 'The Captain', who looked like a Mexican. I learned later that he was from St. Louis and had been in Mexico in some bandit gang or the other. 'You keep an eye on young Sauerkraut,' Conny told him. The Captain gave me two passwords, the names of flowers, 'phlox' and 'daisy'.

As we travelled through the streets of Chicago to Capone's home I noticed that we were not bound towards one of the posh residential districts, where I had supposed Capone would live, but towards the better part of the business section. We stopped in front of a three-storey building, where no one would have expected to find a private apartment. Two small signs announced that the building contained the offices of a wholesale stocking firm and of 'Smith and Weber'. As I found later, both firms actually existed and did a regular and good business. But the stocking agency served as a weapon storage place for Capone while 'Smith and Weber' were used as a secret address.

We entered the vestibule of the building. A giant African-American operated the extraordinarily big elevator that we found there. I saw no signs of any staircase, and learned later that there was none. As the elevator moved slowly upwards the man made a telephone call from a phone in the elevator.

We arrived at the third floor and stepped out into a tiny

vestibule that scarcely held the eight of us. A massive bronze door barred our way. It had neither lock nor handle on the outside, and could be opened only from within. Suddenly, without a sound, the door opened, sliding into the wall.

A man of Asian nationality and of uncertain age, dressed in dark-blue livery received us. He led us down a corridor, walking noiselessly on cork soles. I tried to imitate his quiet walk; the others tramped along noisily. As we passed through the hall I looked into one room, through the open door. It was furnished with Renaissance furniture. Then we came to a large, well-lit room at the end of the corridor, furnished likewise. Before the big window, at a huge desk, sat a man, with his back to us. I saw that his head was big, humpy, covered by thick black hair. His head was slightly drawn in between the wide shoulders and rested on a short, bull-like neck.

He rose quietly and, for his weight, lightly. He was about five-feet-seven in height. He walked towards us, smiling, taking long, sure strides. He wore a dark suit, elegantly cut, a flashy tie. He greeted all of us, shaking hands all round, first with Conny and the last one was me.

'You are the German boy?' he asked, in a deep, almost hoarse, voice.

'Yes.'

'Were you in the War?' he continued, asking the same question which Alphonso had asked.

'I was too young.'

'The Germans were good fighters,' he remarked.

Most of the pictures of Capone do not show him as he is. True, he did have a certain animal-like wildness in his face, a wildness reminiscent of a wild-cat. He carried his head erect, despite his short neck. He had strongly protruding cheek-bones, an energetic chin, hair slightly receding, black bushy eyebrows almost joined together. His eyes were small, with a very white background that offset brown pupils. His glance was piercing, strong, cunning, and perhaps a trifle sad. His nose was flat, his mouth was big, broad, thick, and his lip curved as if in scorn. His teeth were white. A scar ran down the length of his left cheek; a scar received in a fight in a Brooklyn bar-room long ago. His face had a dull dark-blue shadow from his heavy beard. He looked distinctly Italian but other blood also flowed in the veins of some of his ancestors.

After greeting us, Capone sat down at his desk and put a menthol cigarette between his lips. He began talking with Conny. The three of us were sent out to wait in another room.

This room was also furnished similarly to the others, and on close examination I found that the furniture was genuine antique. All around us were bookcases; I found later that it was Capone's library.

'We can't hear anything of what's going on in the other room,' I said to one man called 'The Count'. 'Supposing Capone wanted us?'

The Count, without a word, pointed to an alarm bell overhead.

I stepped up to the bookcases to see what Capone liked to read. The Count smiled. 'You'll find the Boss has good taste,' he said.

First I saw a big collection of erotic books. There were a lot of books which were valuable old prints. I saw a large number of books on Napoleon, some of them in expensive leather binding. *Quotes by Napoleon,* seemed to have been often read. There were thumbed-through books on every possible subject—science, business management, salesmanship, anarchism, naval warfare, architecture, grape-growing, history of the Civil War; books by Roosevelt, Ford, Mark Twain, Upton Sinclair, Stevenson,

Hergeshimer, and Karl Marx. Everything was in English except for some of the French erotic literature.

I was glancing through one of the books when the door behind us suddenly opened and Capone burst into the room, livid. He waved a crumpled newspaper.

'It's enough to make you go nuts,' he said, 'when fellows like Michael Hughes use my name to gain shabby publicity for themselves. I have never seen this fellow Hughes, and he had better not let me see him. He can be fresh, but not more than that. Look at this!' He pointed to a headline:

'Hughes, police commissioner, says he has stopped work of Capone and gang in Chicago and Cook County!'

'All I can say is that if he wants to do that he'll have to get up a hell of a lot earlier,' Capone said, dropping into an arm-chair. He continued to fume. A telephone call took him back into his room.

'I wouldn't like to be in Hughes's shoes,' I said to the other two in the room.

'You wouldn't risk much at that,' said the other man, a tall blond called Andy. 'You probably don't know who made this Hughes Police Commissioner. Big Bill Thompson did it—Big Bill, the new mayor of Chicago, who is going to keep King George's snout out of American affairs, and who declared just yesterday that he was as wet and wetter than the middle of the Atlantic Ocean. And who had Big Bill elected? Who defeated Dever? The Boss!'

'That's right,' said the Count.

'Yah,' Andy continued. 'Then this louse Thompson, after the election, said that he wouldn't prosecute small alcohol cookers and bootleggers, but that he would drive "Crime and Capone" out of Chicago. That's us! Drive out those who had him elected! A lot of words—that's all, and the same with this

Hughes. They just get publicity this way. We're here, and we stay here—no matter what these little newspaper fleas may write. But what makes the Boss sore is that Hughes used to be one of the best customers in Higgins's money-lending bureau. If the Boss wanted to, he could write a nice little piece about Hughes for the papers.'

'Hughes is in luck,' said the Count. 'The Boss has more to worry about now than about him.'

'Yes,' said Andy. 'There are strange gunmen in this city—Aiello's men, from St. Louis, New York, and Cleveland, who would like to get Capone. The gangster armistice is perforated like the hide of a hijacker. Competition for business is active again, and some of these strangers have even dared to turn up in the 42nd and 43rd Wards—Capone's own district! Hymie Weiss, the only one who could have hurt us, is dead. The Boss today controls all that was allotted to him by the armistice, and probably more, but new gangs with ambitions are being formed out of the remnants of the old O'Bannion crowd, and their goal is to get Capone.'

'And just think,' the Count chimed in, 'we can't ask Mr Hughes to protect us!'

'Him?' Andy asked. 'We can look out for ourselves. Hughes doesn't know anything. Wouldn't the famous Mr Hughes like to know the identity of the well-dressed man with the big diamond ring on his hand and the roll of bills in his pocket who was found dead in the Loop the other day? Ten bullets in his body. Hughes couldn't give you his name any more than he could name the man who shot him. To hell with Hughes! We've got these other mugs to look out for.'

'During the armistice not a shot was fired in Chicago for ninety days, Sauerkraut,' the Count explained. 'Those days are over,' Andy added. 'We may have some hot times again.'

They laughed, and I laughed with them. I didn't quite understand all this, for some of the links were missing. I had to understand how all these things fitted together. Sooner than I hoped, I was to find out—in theory and in practice.

The Captain stepped into the room.

'Hurry up, boys. The Boss is going to visit "Poor Mike's." Is everything ready, German?'

In two seconds we were in the hall. Without a sound the bronze door opened. At a signal the Count and I jumped on the small platform between the door and the elevator. Immediately after us the Boss stepped out and behind him the others. Capone was laughing.

At the kerb a dark-blue sedan was waiting. Capone jumped lightly into it. The Captain put George in the front seat, beside the chauffeur, while he, Andy, and I sat in the rear with Capone. Two men, mounted on motorcycles, followed right behind us. 'You watch the left side of the road,' the Captain said curtly to me.

I sat in my place, my eyes focused on the road as we sped by, ready to shoot at the slightest sign of trouble. But there was nothing suspicious in sight. With great speed we travelled along the Lake boulevard, bound for out of town.

'Lovely weather,' said Capone suddenly.

We 'Yessed' him and continued our silent watch.

We left the city and hit the open road. On each side were trees and shrubbery. We had not gone far when *it* happened, and it happened so quickly that it is difficult to remember all the details.

I was conscious of a fast car overtaking us. As it passed, the car seemed to spurt streaks of fire. The noise of shooting rose above the whirr of the motor.

At the first shot Andy and the Captain threw themselves

on Capone. I also covered him instinctively. Andy had one hand free and was firing at the black car that stayed beside us. I did the same.

Suddenly George, in front, slumped in his seat, and blood spurted from his head. A moment later our chauffeur dropped over the wheel. Our car swerved, skidded, and turned over. And all this happened in about twenty seconds!

The time it took us to scramble out of our car seemed like a torturous eternity. Once out we kept shooting at the black car, now slowing down ahead of us, but we were badly covered. We made for the trees beside the road. The road which had been full of passing cars a few moments before was now desolate. A hundred feet away the black car was stopping. The two motorcycle men had not chased it, but were with us.

'Come on to the black car,' Capone ordered, taking command.

The six of us, keeping as well covered as possible, sneaked from tree to tree and from bush to bush, firing at the car as we advanced. One of the motorcycle men, Sascha, led the line. He was the first to reach the last tree before the car. He acted as a feeler, a periscope. He stuck his head out from behind the tree, but jerked it back quickly as if he did not trust the seeming lack of gun fire from the black car. Then with one step he jumped at the car. I loaded my gun for the third time. Capone, in front of me, was hurrying to the car, his face as emotionless as a steel plate.

We had nothing further to fear from the black car. We peered inside. Nothing stirred within. There lay four men in little pools of blood. We did not recognize any of them.

'These men are not gangsters,' Capone said suddenly, breaking a long silence. 'In the first place, they didn't work quickly and smoothly enough to be gangsters. Search them quickly.'

For the first time in my life I searched the pockets of a corpse. I found nothing. There was nothing to identify the men in their pockets or otherwise.

'Let's get to the hospital with our men,' Capone commanded. 'We have to get away from here immediately.'

It was dangerous for us to stay around. We found that our chauffeur was dead, so we left him in the overturned car. Sascha and George were badly wounded. I had been slightly grazed by a bullet. I carried George on my shoulder who was unconscious and weighed like a sack of lead: We had to move slowly along the road. Not a person was in sight, although the road was lined with houses. Strangly enough there was no sign of the police either.

'Where can Commissioner Hughes be?' Capone asked mockingly.

Suddenly a taxi turned from a side street into the road we were walking down. Sighting us, the car made a desperate attempt to turn and head in the other direction. We must have looked pretty wild, or perhaps the driver saw me carrying George and thought that he was dead. Andy fired a shot into the air and the taxi stopped.

The Boss went to the driver and handed him a ten-dollar bill. The Captain opened the door and we got in. We put George between Andy and myself. The taxi-driver disappeared and the Captain drove.

After ten minutes George showed some signs of consciousness. Andy pulled out a flask and poured whisky down his mouth.

Suddenly George put his hand to his head.

'Where the hell is my left ear?' he asked angrily.

It was gone—shot off.

George cursed so completely and satisfactorily that we knew

he was in no serious danger.

'Better have no ears at all,' Andy said to him, 'than to have the kind you had that stick out at right angles. No wonder your left ear stopped a bullet.'

I was not too worried about George now. But Sascha was in a serious condition. I asked Andy if the hospital to which we were going was dependable, meaning whether it took good care of its patients. Andy misunderstood me.

'You bet it's dependable,' he said. 'We control it. No police can get into it.'

George seemed to have recovered, but Sascha was groaning. Andy tried to fix him up with an emergency bandage, but his pain was excruciating. The second half of our journey was covered in silence.

Capone had said nothing the whole way. Suddenly he let out one loud curse, and added, 'I know! We received threats from the Ku-Klux-Klan. It wants to rid America of me. Well, they'll have to learn to shoot better first.' After this he said no more.

The hospital was an attractive two-storey building, built in a colonial style a distance away from the road. Two nurses took charge of George and Sascha. It was in this hospital that 'Poor Mike' lay. Capone asked for the number of his room and went up to it with the Captain. We stayed downstairs and drank whisky.

In ten minutes the Boss was back. He looked gloomy and silent and none of us dared question him. We were in the car and on our way to Chicago before he said a word.

'Poor Mike is dead,' he stated simply. 'He was a good gunman.'

THE INTERRUPTION

W.W. Jacobs

The last of the funeral guests had gone, and Spencer Goddard, in decent black, sat alone in his small, well-furnished study. There was a queer sense of freedom in the house since the coffin had left it; the coffin which was now hidden in its solitary grave beneath the yellow earth. The air, which for the last three days had seemed stale and contaminated, now smelt fresh and clean. He went to the open window and, looking into the fading light of the autumn day, took a deep breath.

He closed the window and, stooping down, put a match to the fire, and, dropping into his easy chair, sat listening to the cheery crackle of the wood. At the age of thirty-eight he had turned over a fresh page. Life, free and unencumbered, was before him. His dead wife's money was at last his, to spend as he pleased instead of being doled out in reluctant driblets.

He turned at a step at the door, and his face assumed the appearance of gravity and sadness it had worn for the last four days. The cook, with the same air of decorous grief, entered the room quietly and, crossing to the mantelpiece, placed upon it a photograph.

'I thought you'd like to have it, sir.' She said, in a low voice, 'to remind you.'

Goddard thanked her, and, rising, took it in his hand and stood regarding it. He noticed with satisfaction that his hand was absolutely steady.

'It is a very good likeness—till she was taken ill,' continued the woman. 'I never saw anybody change so sudden.'

'The nature of her disease, Hannah,' said her master.

The woman nodded, and, dabbing at her eyes with her handkerchief, stood regarding him.

'Is there anything you want?' he inquired, after a time.

She shook her head. 'I can't believe she's gone,' she said, in a low voice. 'Every now and then I have a queer feeling that she's still here—'

'It's your nerves,' said her master sharply.

'—and wanting to tell me something.'

By a great effort Goddard refrained from looking at her.

'Nerves,' he said again. 'Perhaps, you ought to have a little holiday. It has been a great strain upon you.'

'You, too, sir,' said the woman respectfully. 'Waiting on her hand and foot as you have done, I can't think how you stood it. If you'd only had a nurse—'

'I preferred to do it myself, Hannah,' said her master. 'If I had had a nurse it would have alarmed her.'

The woman assented. 'And, they are always peeking and prying into that doesn't concern them,' she added. 'Always think they know more than the doctors do.'

Goddard turned a slow look upon her. The tall, angular figure was standing in an attitude of respectful attention; the cold, slaty-brown eyes were cast down, the sullen face expressionless.

'She couldn't have had a better doctor,' he said, looking at the fire again. 'No man could have done more for her.'

'And, nobody could have done more for her than you did,

sir,' was the reply 'There's few husbands that would have done what you did.'

Goddard stiffened in his chair. 'That will do, Hannah,' he said curtly.

'Or, done it so well,' said the woman, with measured slowness.

With a strange, sinking sensation, her master paused to regain his control. Then he turned and eyed her steadily. 'Thank you,' he said slowly; 'you mean well, but at present I cannot discuss it.'

For some time after the door had closed behind her he sat in deep thought. The feeling of well-being of a few minutes before had vanished, leaving in its place an apprehension which he refused to consider, but which would not be allayed. He thought over his actions of the last few weeks, carefully, and could remember no flaw. His wife's illness, the doctor's diagnosis, his own solicitous care, were all in keeping with the ordinary. He tried to remember the woman's exact words—her manner. Something had shown him Fear. What?

He could have laughed at his fears next morning. The dining-room was full of sunshine and the fragrance of coffee and bacon was in the air. Better still, a worried and commonplace Hannah. Worried over two eggs with false birth-certificates, over the vendor of which she became almost lyrical.

'The bacon is excellent,' said her smiling master, 'so is the coffee; but your coffee always is.'

Hannah smiled in return, and, taking fresh eggs from a rosy-cheeked maid, put them before him.

A pipe, followed by a brisk walk, cheered him still further. He came home glowing with exercise and again possessed with that sense of freedom and freshness. He went into the garden—now his own—planned alterations.

After lunch he went over the house. The windows of his

wife's bedroom were open and the room neat and airy. His glance wandered from the made-up bed to the brightly polished furniture. Then he went to the dressing-table and opened the drawers, searching each in turn. With the exception of a few odds and ends they were empty. He went out on to the landing and called for Hannah.

'Do you know whether your mistress locked up any of her things?' he inquired.

'What things?' said the woman.

'Well, her jewellery mostly,'

'Oh.' Hannah smiled. 'She gave it all to me,' she said quietly. Goddard checked an exclamation. His heart was beating nervously, but he spoke sternly.

'When?'

'Just before she died—of gastro-enteritis,' said the woman. There was a long silence. He turned and with great care mechanically closed the drawers of the dressing-table. The tilted glass showed him the pallor of his face, and he spoke without turning round.

'That is all right, then,' he said huskily. 'I only wanted to know what had become of it. I thought, perhaps, Milly—'

Hannah shook her head. 'Milly's all right,' she said, with a strange smile. 'She's as honest as we are. Is there anything more you want, sir?'

She closed the door behind her with the quietness of the well-trained servant; Goddard, steadying himself with his hand on the rail of the bed, stood looking into the future.

II

The days passed monotonously, as they pass with a man in prison. Gone was the sense of freedom and the idea of a wider life Instead of a cell, a house with ten rooms—but Hannah, the jailer, guarding each one. Respectful and attentive, in the model servant he saw every word a threat against his liberty—his life. In the sullen face and cold eyes he saw her knowledge of power; in her solicitude for his comfort and approval, a sardonic jest. It was the master playing at being the servant. The years of unwilling servitude were over, but she felt her way carefully with infinite zest in the game. Warped and bitter, with a cleverness which had never before had scope, she had entered into her kingdom. She took it little by little, savouring every morsel.

'I hope I've done right, sir,' she said one morning. 'I have given Milly notice.'

Goddard looked up from his paper. 'Isn't she satisfactory?' he inquired.

'Not to my thinking, sir,' said the woman. 'And, she says she is coming to see you about it. I told her that would be no good.'

'I had better see her and hear what she has to say,' said her master.

'Of course, if you wish to,' said Hannah; 'only, after giving her notice, if she doesn't go I shall. I should be sorry to go—I've been very comfortable here—but it's either her or me.'

'I should be sorry to lose you,' said Goddard in a hopeless voice.

'Thank you, sir,' said Hannah, 'I'm sure I've tried to do my best. I've been with you some time now—and I know all your little ways. I expect I understand you better than anybody else would. I do all I can to make you comfortable.'

'Very well, I leave it to you,' said Goddard in a voice which strove to be brisk and commanding. 'You have my permission to dismiss her.'

'There's another thing I wanted to see you about,' said Hannah; 'my wages. I was going to ask for a raise, seeing that

I'm really housekeeper here now.'

'Certainly,' said her master, considering, 'that only seems fair. Let me see—what are you getting?'

'Thirty-six.'

Goddard reflected for a moment, and then turned with a benevolent smile. 'Very well,' he said cordially, 'I'll make it forty-two. That's ten shillings a month more.'

'I was thinking of a hundred,' said Hannah dryly.

The significance of the demand appalled him. 'Rather a big jump,' he said at last, 'I really don't know that I—'

'It doesn't matter,' said Hannah, 'I thought I was worth it—to you—that's all. You know best. Some people might think I was worth two hundred. That's a bigger jump, but after all a big jump is better than—'

She broke off and tittered. Goddard eyed her.

'—than a big drop,' she concluded.

Her master's face set. The lips almost disappeared and something came into the pale eyes that was revolting. Still eyeing her, he rose and approached her. She stood her ground and met him eye to eye.

'You are jocular,' he said at last.

'Short life and a merry one,' said the woman.

'Mine or yours?'

'Both, perhaps,' was the reply.

'If—if I give you a hundred,' said Goddard, moistening his lips, 'that ought to make your life merrier, at any rate.'

Hannah nodded. 'Merry and long, perhaps,' she said slowly. 'I'm careful, you know—very careful.'

'I am sure you are,' said Goddard, his face relaxing.

'Careful what I eat and drink, I mean,' said the woman eyeing him steadily.

'That is wise,' he said slowly. 'I am myself—that is why I

am paying a good cook a large salary. But don't overdo things, Hannah; don't kill the goose that lays the golden eggs.'

'I am not likely to do that,' she said coldly. 'Live and let live; that is my motto. Some people have different ones. But I'm careful; nobody won't catch me napping. I've left a letter with my sister, in case.'

Goddard turned slowly and in a casual fashion put the flowers straight in a bowl on the table, and, wandering to the window, looked out. His face was white again and his hands trembled. 'To be opened after my death,' continued Hannah. 'I don't believe in doctors—not after what I've seen of them—I don't think they know enough; so if I die I shall be examined. I've given good reasons.'

'And, suppose,' said Goddard, coming from the window, 'suppose she is curious, and opens it before you die?'

'We must chance that,' said Hannah, shrugging her shoulders; 'but I don't think she will. I sealed it up with sealing-wax, with a mark on it.'

'She might open it and say nothing about it,' persisted her master.

An unwholesome grin spread slowly over Hannah's features. 'I should know it soon enough,' she declared boisterously, 'and so would other people. Lord! There would be an upset! Chidham would have something to talk about for once. We should be in the paper—both of us.'

Goddard forced a smile. 'Dear me?' he said gently. 'Your pen seems to be a dangerous weapon, Hannah, but I hope that the need to open it will not happen for another fifty years. You look well and strong.'

The woman nodded. 'I don't take up my troubles before they come,' she said, with a satisfied air; 'but there's no harm in trying to prevent them coming. Prevention is better than cure.'

'Exactly,' said her master; 'and, by the way, there's no need for this little financial arrangement to be known by anybody else. I might become unpopular with my neighbours for setting a bad example. Of course, I am giving you this sum because I really think you are worth it.'

'I'm sure you do,' said Hannah. 'I'm not sure I ain't worth more but this'll do to go on with. I shall get a girl for less than we are paying Milly, and that'll be another little bit extra for me.'

'Certainly,' said Goddard, and smiled again.

'Come to think of it,' said Hannah, pausing at the door, 'I ain't sure I shall get anybody else; then there'll be more than ever for me. If I do the work I might as well have the money.'

Her master nodded, and, left to himself, sat down to think out a position which was as intolerable as it was dangerous. At a great risk he had escaped from the dominion of one woman only to fall, bound and helpless, into the hands of another. However vague and unconvincing the suspicions of Hannah might be, they would be sufficient. Evidence could be unearthed. Cold with fear one moment, and hot with fury the next, he sought in vain for some avenue of escape. It was his brain against that of a cunning, illiterate fool; a fool whose malicious stupidity only added to his danger. And she drank. With largely increased wages she would drink more and his very life might depend upon a hiccupped boast. It was clear that she was enjoying her supremacy; later on her vanity would urge her to display it before others. He might have to obey the crack of her whip before witnesses, and that would cut off all possibility of escape.

He sat with his head in his hands. There must be a way out and he must find it—soon. He must find it before gossip began; before the changed position of master and servant lent colour to her story when that story became known. Shaking with fury, he thought of her lean, ugly throat and the joy of choking her life out with his fingers. He started suddenly, and took a quick breath. No, not fingers—a rope.

III

Bright and cheerful outside and with his friends, in the house he was quiet and submissive. Milly had gone, and, if the service was poorer and the rooms neglected, he gave no sign. If a bell remained unanswered he made no complaint, and to studied insolence turned the other cheek of politeness. When at this tribute to her power the woman smiled, he smiled in return. A smile which, for all its disarming softness, left her vaguely uneasy.

'I'm not afraid of you,' she said once, with a menacing air.

'I hope not,' said Goddard in a slightly surprised voice.

'Some people might be, but I'm not,' she declared. 'If anything happened to me—'

'Nothing could happen to such a careful woman as you are,' he said, smiling again. 'You ought to live to ninety—with luck.'

It was clear to him that the situation was getting on his nerves. Unremembered but terrible dreams haunted his sleep. Dreams in which some great, inevitable disaster was always pressing upon him, although he could never discover what it was. Each morning he awoke unrefreshed to face another day of torment. He could not meet the woman's eyes for fear of revealing the threat that was in his own.

Delay was dangerous and foolish. He had thought out every move in that contest of wits which was to remove the shadow of the rope from his own neck and place it about that of the woman. There was a little risk, but the stake was a big one. He had but to set the ball rolling and others would keep it on its course. It was time to act.

He came in a little jaded from his afternoon walk, and left

his tea untouched. He ate but little dinner, and, sitting hunched up over the fire, told the woman that he had taken a slight chill. Her concern, he felt grimly, might have been greater if she had known the cause.

He was no better next day, and after lunch called in to consult his doctor. He left with a clean bill of health except for a slight digestive derangement, the remedy for which he took away with him in a bottle. For two days he swallowed one tablespoonful three times a day in water, without result, then he took to his bed.

'A day or two in bed won't hurt you,' said the doctor. 'Show me that tongue of yours again.'

'But what is the matter with me, Roberts?' inquired the patient.

The doctor pondered. 'Nothing to trouble about—nerves a bit wrong—digestion a little bit impaired. You'll be all right in a day or two.'

Goddard nodded. So far, so good; Roberts had not outlived his usefulness. He smiled grimly after the doctor had left at the surprise he was preparing for him. A little rough on Roberts and his professional reputation, perhaps, but these things could not be avoided.

He lay back and visualized the programme. A day or two longer, getting gradually worse, then a little sickness. After that a nervous, somewhat shame-faced patient hinting at things. His food had a queer taste—he felt worse after taking it; he knew it was ridiculous, still—there was some of his beef-tea he had put aside, perhaps the doctor would like to examine it, and the medicine? Secretions, too; perhaps he would like to see those?

Propped on his elbow, he stared fixedly at the wall. There would be a trace—a faint trace—of arsenic in the secretions. There would be more than a trace in the other things. An attempt to poison him would be clearly indicated, and—his wife's symptoms had resembled his own—let Hannah get out of the web he was spinning if she could. As for the letter she had threatened him with, let her produce it; it could only recoil upon herself. Fifty letters could not save her from the doom he was preparing for her. It was her life or his, and he would show no mercy. For three days he doctored himself with sedulous care, watching himself anxiously meanwhile. His nerve was going and he knew it. Before him was the strain of the discovery, the arrest, and the trial. The gruesome business of his wife's death. A long business. He would wait no longer, and he would open the proceedings with dramatic suddenness.

It was between nine and ten o'clock at night when he rang his bell, and it was not until he had rung four times that he heard the heavy steps of Hannah mounting the stairs.

'What d'you want'?' she demanded, standing in the doorway.

'I'm very ill,' he said gasping. 'Run for the doctor. Quick!' The woman stared at him in genuine amazement. 'What, at this time o'night?' she exclaimed. 'Not likely.'

'I'm dying!' said Goddard in a broken voice.

'Not you,' she said roughly. 'You'll be better in the morning.'

'I'm dying,' he repeated. 'Go—for—the—doctor.'

The woman hesitated. The rain beat in heavy squalls against the window, and the doctor's house was a mile distant on the lonely road. She glanced at the figure on the bed.

'I should catch my death o' cold,' she grumbled.

She stood sullenly regarding him. He certainly looked very ill, and his death would by no means benefit her. She listened, scowling, to the wind and the rain.

'All right,' she said at last, and went noisily from the room.

His face set in a mirthless smile, he heard her bustling about below. The front-door slammed violently and he was alone.

He waited for a few minutes and then, getting out of bed, put on his dressing-gown and set about his preparations. With a steady hand he added a little white powder to the remains of his beef-tea and to the contents of his bottle of medicine. He stood listening a moment at some faint sound from below, and, having satisfied himself, lit a candle and made his way to Hannah's room. For a space he stood irresolute, looking about him. Then he opened one of the drawers and, placing the broken packet of powder under a pile of clothing at the back, made his way back to bed.

He was disturbed to find he was trembling with excitement and nervousness. He longed for tobacco, but that was impossible. To reassure himself he began to rehearse his conversation with the doctor, and again he thought over every possible complication. The scene with the woman would be terrible: he would have to be too ill to take any part in it. The less he said the better. Others would do all that was necessary.

He lay for a long time listening to the sound of the wind and the rain. Inside, the house seemed unusually quiet, and with an odd sensation he suddenly realized that it was the first time he had been alone in it since his wife's death. He remembered that she would have to be disturbed. The thought was unwelcome. He did not want her to be disturbed. Let the dead sleep.

He sat up in bed and drew his watch from beneath the pillow, Hannah ought to have been back before; in any case she could not be long now. At any moment he might hear her key in the lock. He lay down again and reminded himself that things were shaping well. He had shaped them, and some of the satisfaction of the artist was his.

The silence was oppressive. The house seemed to be listening, waiting. He looked at his watch again and wondered, with a curse, what had happened to the woman. It was clear that the doctor must be out, but that was no reason for her delay. It was close on midnight, and the atmosphere of the house seemed in some strange fashion to be brooding and hostile.

In a lull in the wind he thought he heard footsteps outside, and his face cleared as he sat up listening for the sound of the key in the door below. In another moment the woman would be in the house and the fears engendered by a disordered fancy would have flown. The sound of the steps had ceased, but he could hear no sound of entrance. Until all hope had gone, he sat listening. He was certain he had heard footsteps. Whose?

Trembling, and haggard he sat waiting, assailed by a crowd of murmuring fears. One whispered that he had failed and would have to pay the penalty of failing; that he had gambled with Death and lost.

By a strong effort he fought down these fancies and, closing his eyes, tried to compose himself to rest. It was evident now that the doctor was out and that Hannah was waiting to return with him in his car. He was frightening himself for nothing. At any moment he might hear the sound of their arrival.

He heard something else, and, sitting up suddenly, tried to think what it was and what had caused it. It was a very faint sound—stealthy. Holding his breath, he waited for it to be repeated. He heard it again, the mere ghost of a sound—the whisper of a sound, but significant as most whispers are.

He wiped his brow with his sleeve and told himself firmly that it was nerves, and nothing but nerves; but, against his will, he still listened. He fancied now that the sound came from his wife's room, the other side of the landing. It increased in loudness and became more insistent, but with his eyes fixed on the door of his room he still kept himself in hand, and tried to listen instead to the wind and the rain.

For a time he heard nothing but that. Then there came a

scraping, scurrying noise from his wife's room, and a sudden, terrific crash.

With a loud scream his nerve broke, and springing from the bed he sped downstairs and, flinging open the front-door, dashed into the night. The door, caught by the wind, slammed behind him.

With his hand holding the garden gate open, ready for further flight, he stood sobbing for breath. His bare feet were bruised and the rain was very cold, but he took no heed. Then he ran a little way along the road and stood for some time, hoping and listening.

He came back slowly. The wind was bitter and he was bitter and he was soaked to the skin. The garden was black and forbidding, and unspeakable horror might be lurking in the bushes. He went up the road again, trembling with cold. Then, in desperation, he passed through the terrors of the garden to the house, only to find the door closed. The porch gave a little protection from the icy rain, but none from the wind, and, shaking in every limb, he leaned in abject misery against the door. He pulled himself together after a time and stumbled round to the back-door. Locked! And, all the lower windows were shuttered. He made his way back to the porch, and, crouching there in hopeless misery, waited for the woman to return.

IV

He had a dim memory when he awoke of somebody questioning him and then of being half-pushed, half-carried upstairs to bed. There was something wrong with his head and his chest, and he was trembling violently, and very cold. Somebody was speaking. 'You must have taken leave of your senses,' said the voice of

Hannah. 'I thought you were dead.'

He forced his eyes to open 'Doctor,' he muttered, 'doctor.'

'Out on a bad case,' said Hannah, 'I waited till I was tired of waiting, and then came along. Good thing for you I did. He'll be round first thing this morning. He ought to be here now.'

She bustled about, tidying up the room, his leaden eyes following her as she collected the beef-tea and a tray and carried them out.

'Nice thing I did yesterday,' she remarked, as she came back. 'Left the missus's bedroom window open. When I opened the door this morning I found that beautiful Chippendale glass of hers had blown off the table and, smashed to pieces. Did you hear it?'

Goddard made no reply. In a confused fashion he was trying to think. Accident or not, the fall of the glass had served its purpose. Were there such things as accident? Or, was Life a puzzle—a puzzle into which every piece was made to fit? Fear and the wind...no: conscience and the wind...had saved the woman. He must get the powder back from her drawer...before she discovered it and denounced him. The medicine...he must remember not to take it...

He was very ill, seriously ill. He must have taken a chill owing to that panic flight into the garden. Why didn't the doctor come? He had come...at last...he was doing something to his chest...it was cold.

Again...the doctor...there was something he wanted to tell him...Hannah and a powder...what was it?

Later on he remembered, together with other things that he had hoped to forget. He lay watching an endless procession of memories, broken at times by a glance at the doctor, the nurse, and Hannah, who were all standing near the bed regarding him. They had been there a long time, and they were all very quiet. The last time he looked at Hannah was the first time for months that he had looked at her without loathing and hatred. Then he knew that he was dying.

THE PERFECT MURDER

Stacy Aumonier

One evening in November two brothers were seated in a little café in the Rue de la Roquette discussing murders. The evening papers lay in front of them, and they all contained a lurid account of a shocking affair in the Landes district, where a charcoal-burner had killed his wife and two children with a hatchet. From discussing this murder in particular they went on to discussing murder in general.

'I've never yet read a murder case without being impressed by the extraordinary clumsiness of it,' remarked Paul, the younger brother. 'Here's this fellow who murders his victims with his own hatchet, leaves his hat behind in the shed, and arrives at a village hard by, with blood on his boots.'

'They lose their heads,' said Henri, the elder. 'In cases like that they are mentally unbalanced, hardly responsible for their actions.'

'Yes,' replied Paul, 'but what impresses me is—what a lot of murders must be done by people who take trouble, who leave not a trace behind.'

Henri shrugged his shoulders. 'I shouldn't think it was so easy, old boy; there's always something that crops up.'

'Nonsense! I'll guarantee there are thousands done every year. If you are living with anyone, for instance, it must be the easiest thing in the world to murder them.'

'How?'

'Oh, some kind of accident—and then you go screaming into the street, "Oh, my poor wife! Help!" You burst into tears, and everyone consoles you. I read of a woman somewhere who murdered her husband by leaving the window near the bed open at night when he was suffering from pneumonia. Who's going to suspect a case like that? Instead of that, people must always select revolvers, or knives, or go and buy poison at the chemist's across the way.'

'It sounds as though you were contemplating a murder yourself,' laughed Henri.

'Well, you never know,' answered Paul; 'circumstances might arise when a murder would be the only way out of a difficulty. If ever my time comes I shall take a lot of trouble about it. I promise you, I shall leave no trace behind.'

As Henri glanced at his brother making this remark, he was struck by the fact that there was indeed nothing irreconcilable between the idea of a murder and the idea of Paul doing it. He was a big, saturnine-looking gentleman with a sallow, dissolute face, framed in a black square beard and swathes of untidy grey hair. His profession was that of a traveller in cheap jewellery, and his business dealings were not always the straightest. Henri shuddered. With his own puny physique, bad health, and vacillating will, he was always dominated by his younger brother. He himself was a clerk in a drapery store, and he had a wife and three children. Paul was unmarried.

The brothers saw a good deal of each other, and were very intimate. But the word friendship would be an extravagant term to apply to their relationship. They were both always hard up, and they borrowed money from each other when every other source failed.

They had no other relatives except a very old uncle and aunt who lived at Chantilly. This uncle and aunt, whose name was Taillandier, were fairly well-off, but they would have little to do with the two nephews. They were occasionally invited there to dinner, but neither Paul nor Henri ever succeeded in extracting a franc out of Uncle Robert. He was a very religious man, hard-fisted, cantankerous and intolerant. His wife was a little more pliable. She was in effect an eccentric. She had spasms of generosity, during which periods both the brothers had, at times, managed to get money out of her. But these were rare occasions. Moreover, the old man kept her so short of cash that she found it difficult to help her nephews even if she desired to.

As stated, the discussion between the two brothers occurred in November. It was presumably forgotten by both of them immediately afterwards. And indeed, there is no reason to believe that it would ever have recurred, except for certain events which followed the sudden death of Uncle Robert in the February of the following year.

In the meantime, the affairs of both Paul and Henri had gone disastrously. Paul had been detected in a dishonest transaction over a paste trinket, and had just been released from a period of imprisonment. The knowledge of this had not reached his uncle before his death. Henri's wife had had another baby, and had been very ill. He was more in debt than ever.

The news of the uncle's death came as a gleam of hope in the darkness of despair. What kind of will had he left? Knowing their uncle, each was convinced that, however it was framed there was likely to be little or nothing for them. However, the old villain might have left them a thousand or two. And in any case, if the money was all left to the wife, here was a possible field of plunder. It need hardly be said that they repaired with all haste to the funeral, and even with greater alacrity to the lawyer's reading of the will.

The will contained surprises both encouraging and discouraging. In the first place, the old man had left a considerably larger fortune than anyone could have anticipated. In the second place, all the money and securities were carefully tied up, and placed under the control of trustees. There were large bequests to religious charities, whilst the residue was held in trust for his wife. But so far as the brothers were concerned the surprise came at the end. On her death this residue was still to be held in trust, but a portion of the interest was to be divided between Henri and Paul, and on their death to go to the Church. The old man had recognized a certain call of the blood after all!

They both behaved with tact and discretion at the funeral, and were extremely sympathetic and solicitous towards Aunt Rosalie, who was too absorbed with her own trouble to take much notice of them. It was only when it came to the reading of the will that their avidity and interest outraged, perhaps, the strict canons of good taste. It was Paul who managed to get it clear from the notary what the exact amount would probably be. Making allowances for fluctuations, accidents and acts of God, on the death of Mme Taillandier, the two brothers would inherit something between eight and ten thousand francs a year each. She was eighty-two and very frail.

The brothers celebrated the good news with a carouse up in Montmartre. Naturally, their chief topic of conversation was how long the old bird would keep on her perch. In any case, it could not be many years. With any luck it might be only a few weeks. The fortune seemed blinding. It would mean comfort and security to the end of their days. The rejoicings were mixed with recriminations against the old man for his stinginess. Why couldn't he have left them a lump sum down now? Why did he want to waste all this good gold on the Church? Why all this trustee business?

There was little they could do but await developments. Except that in the meantime—after a decent interval—they might try and touch the old lady for a bit. They parted, and the next day set about their business in cheerier spirits.

For a time they were extremely tactful. They made formal calls on Aunt Rosalie, inquiring after her health, and offering their services in any capacity whatsoever. But at the end of a month Henri called hurriedly one morning, and after the usual professions of solicitude asked his aunt if she could possibly lend him one hundred and twenty francs to pay the doctor who had attended his wife and baby. She lent him forty, grumbling at his foolishness at having children he could not afford to keep. A week later came Paul with a story about being robbed by a client. He wanted a hundred. She lent him ten.

When these appeals had been repeated three or four times, and received similar treatment—and sometimes no treatment at all—the old lady began to get annoyed. She was becoming more and more eccentric. She now had a companion, an angular, middle-aged woman named Mme Chavanne, who appeared like a protecting goddess. Sometimes when the brothers called, Mme Chavanne would say that Mme Taillandier was too unwell to see anyone. If this news had been true it would have been good news indeed, but the brothers suspected that it was all pre-arranged. Two years went by, and they both began to despair.

'She may live to a hundred,' said Paul.

'We shall die of old age, first,' grumbled Henri.

It was difficult to borrow money on the strength of the will. In the first place, their friends were more of the borrowing than the lending class. And, anyone who had a little was suspicious of the story, and wanted all kinds of securities. It was Paul who first thought of going to an insurance company to try to raise money on the reversionary interest. They did succeed in the end in getting an insurance company to advance them two thousand francs each, but the negotiations took five months to complete, and by the time they had insured their lives, paid the lawyer's fees and paid for the various deeds and stamps, and signed some thirty or forty forms, each man only received a little over a thousand francs, which was quickly lost in paying accrued debts and squandering the remainder. Their hopes were raised by the dismissal of Mme Chavanne, only to be lowered again by the arrival of an even more aggressive companion. The companions came and went with startling rapidity. None of them could stand for any time the old lady's eccentricity and ill-temper. The whole of the staff was always being changed. The only one who remained loyal all through was the portly cook, Ernestine. Even this may have been due to the fact that she never came in touch with her mistress. She was an excellent cook, and she never moved from the kitchen. Moreover, the cooking required by Mme Taillandier was of the simplest nature, and she seldom entertained. And, she hardly ever left her apartment. Any complaints that were made were made through the housekeeper, and the complaints and their retaliations became mellowed in the process; for Ernestine also had a temper of her own.

Nearly another year passed before what appeared to Paul to be a mild stroke of good fortune came his way. Things had been going from bad to worse. Neither of the brothers was in a position to lend a sou to the other. Henri's family was becoming a greater drag, and people were not buying Paul's trinkets.

One day, during an interview with his aunt—Paul had been trying to borrow more money—he fainted in her presence. It is difficult to know what it was about this act which affected the old lady, but she ordered him to be put to bed in one of the rooms of the villa. Possibly, she jumped to the conclusion that he had fainted from lack of food—which was not true, Paul never went without food and drink—and she suddenly realized that after all he was her husband's sister's son. He must certainly have looked pathetic, this white-faced man, well past middle age, and broken in life. Whatever it was, she showed a broad streak of compassion for him. She ordered her servants to look after him, and to allow him to remain until she countermanded the order.

Paul, who had certainly felt faint, but had quickly seized the occasion to make it as dramatic as possible, saw in this an opportunity to wheedle his way into his aunt's favours. His behaviour was exemplary. The next morning, looking very white and shaky, he visited her, and asked her to allow him to go, as he had no idea of abusing her hospitality. If he had taken up the opposite attitude she would probably have turned him out, but because he suggested going, she ordered him to stop. During daytime he went about his dubious business, but he continued to return there at night to sleep, and to enjoy a good dinner cooked by the admirable Ernestine. He was in clover.

Henri was naturally envious when he heard of his brother's good fortune. And, Paul was fearful that Henri would spoil the whole game by going and throwing a fit himself in the presence of the aunt. But this, of course, would have been too obvious and foolish for even Henri to consider seriously. And, he racked his brains for some means of inveigling the old lady. Every plan he put forth, however, Paul sat upon. He was quite comfortable himself, and he didn't see the point of his brother butting in.

'Besides,' he said, 'she may turn me out any day. Then you can have your shot.'

They quarrelled about this, and did not see each other for some time. One would have thought that Henri's appeal to Mme Taillandier would have been stronger than Paul's. He was a struggling individual, with a wife and four children. Paul was a notorious ne'er-do-well, and he had no attachments. Nevertheless, the old lady continued to support Paul. Perhaps, it was because he was a big man, and she liked big men. Her husband had been a man of fine physique. Henri was puny, and she despised him. She had never had children of her own, and she disliked children. She was always upbraiding Henri and his wife for their fecundity. Any attempt to pander to her emotions through the sentiment of childhood failed. She would not have the children in her house. And, any small acts of charity which she bestowed upon them, seemed to be done more with the idea of giving her an opportunity to inflict her sarcasm and venom upon them than out of kindness of heart.

In Paul, on the other hand, she seemed to find something slightly attractive. She sometimes sent for him, and he, all agog— expecting to get his notice to quit—would be agreeably surprised to find that, on the contrary, she had some little commission she wished him to execute. And, you may rest assured that he never failed to make a few francs out of all these occasions. The notice to quit did not come. It may be—poor deluded woman—that she regarded him as some kind of protection. He was, in any case, the only 'man' who slept under her roof.

At first she seldom spoke to him, but as time went on she would sometimes send for him to relieve her loneliness. Nothing could have been more ingratiating than Paul's manners in these knowing circumstances. He talked expansively about politics, beforehand his aunt's views, and just what she would like him to say. Her eyesight was very bad, and he would read her the news of the day, and tell her what was happening in Paris.

He humoured her every whim. He was astute enough to see that it would be foolish and dangerous to attempt to borrow money for the moment. He was biding his time, and trying to think out the most profitable plan of campaign. There was no immediate hurry. His bed was comfortable, and Ernestine's cooking was excellent.

In another year's time, he had established himself as quite one of the permanent householders. He was consulted about the servants, and the doctors, and the management of the house, everything except the control of money, which was jealously guarded by a firm of lawyers. Many a time he would curse his uncle's foresight. The old man's spirit seemed to be hovering in the dim recesses of the over-crowded rooms, mocking him. For the old lady, eccentric and foolish in many ways, kept a strict check upon her dividends. It was her absorbing interest in life, that and an old grey perroquet, which she treated like a child. Its name was Anna, and it used to walk up and down her table at mealtimes and feed off her own plate. Finding himself so firmly entrenched Paul's assurance gradually increased. He began to treat his aunt as an equal, and sometimes even to contradict her, and she did not seem to resent it.

In the meantime, Henri was eating his heart out with jealousy and sullen rage. The whole thing was unfair. He occasionally saw Paul, who boasted openly of his strong position in the Taillandier household, and he would not believe that Paul was not getting money out of the old lady as well as board and lodging. With no additional expenses, Paul was better dressed than he used to be, and he looked fatter and better in health. All—or nearly all—of Henri's appeals, although pitched in a most pathetic key, were rebuffed. He felt a bitter hatred against his aunt, his brother, and life in general. If only she would die! What was the good of life to a woman at eighty-five or six?

And, there was he—four young children, clamouring for food, and clothes, and the ordinary decent comforts. And, there was Paul, idling his days away at cafés and his nights at cabarets—nothing to do, and no responsibilities.

Meeting Paul one day, he said:

'I say, old boy, couldn't you spring me a hundred francs? I haven't the money to pay my rent next week.'

'She gives me nothing,' replied Paul.

Henri did not believe this, but it would be undiplomatic to quarrel. He said:

'Aren't there—isn't there some little thing lying about the villa you could slip in your pocket? We could sell it, see? Go shares. I'm desperately pushed.'

Paul looked down his nose. Name of a pig! Did Henri think he had never thought of that? Many and many a time, the temptation had come to him. But no; every few months people came from the lawyer's office, and the inventory of the whole household was checked. The servants could not be suspected. They were not selected without irreproachable characters. If he were suspected—well, all kinds of unpleasant things might crop up. Oh, no, he was too well off where he was. The game was to lie in wait. The old lady simply must die soon. She had even been complaining of her chest that morning. She was always playing with the perroquet. Somehow this bird got on Paul's nerves. He wanted to wring its neck. He imitated the way she would say, 'There's a pretty lady! Oh, my sweet! Another nice grape for my little one. There's a pretty lady!' He told Henri all about this, and the elder brother went on his way with a grunt that only conveyed doubt and suspicion.

In view of this position, it seemed strange that in the end, it was Paul who was directly responsible for the dénouement in the Taillandier household. His success went to his rather weak head like wine. He began to swagger and buster and abuse his aunt's hospitality. And, curiously enough, the more he advanced the further she withdrew. The eccentric old lady seemed to be losing her powers of resistance so far as he was concerned. And, he began to borrow small sums of money from her, and, as she acquiesced so readily, to increase his demands. He let his travelling business go, and sometimes he would get lost for days at a time. He would spend his time at the races, and drinking with doubtful acquaintances in obscure cafés. Sometimes he won, but in the majority of cases he lost. He ran up bills and got into debt. By cajoling small sums out of his aunt he kept his debtors at bay for nearly nine months.

But one evening he came to see Henri in a great state of distress. His face, which had taken on a healthier glow when he first went to live with his aunt, had become puffy and livid. His eyes were bloodshot.

'Old boy,' he said, 'I'm at my wits' end. I've got to find seven thousand francs by the twenty-first of the month, or they're going to foreclose. How do you stand? I'll pay you back.'

To try to borrow money from Henri was like appealing to the desert for a cooling draught. He also had to find money by the twenty-first, and he was overdrawn at the bank. They exchanged confidences, and in their mutual distress they felt sorry for each other and for themselves. It was a November evening, and the rain was driving along the boulevards in fitful gusts. After trudging a long way they turned into a little café in the Rue de la Roquette, and sat down and ordered two cognacs. The café was almost deserted. A few men in mackintoshes were scattered around reading the evening papers. They sat at a marble table in the corner and tried to think of ways and means. But after a time, a silence fell between them. There seemed nothing more to suggest. They could hear the rain beating on the skylight. An old man, four tables away, was poring over *La Patrie*.

Suddenly, Henri looked furtively around the room and clutched his brother's arm.

'Paul!' he whispered.

'What is it?'

'Do you remember—it has all come back to me—suddenly— one night, a night something like this—it must be give or take, six years ago—we were seated here in this same café—do you remember?'

'No. I don't remember. What was it?'

'It was the night of that murder in the Landes district. We got talking about—don't you remember?'

Paul scratched his temple and sipped the cognac. Henri leant closer to him.

'You said—you said that if you lived with anyone, it was the easiest thing in the world to murder them. An accident, you know. And, you go screaming into the street—'

Paul started, and stared at his brother, who continued:

'You said that if ever you—you had to do it, you would guarantee that you would take every trouble. You wouldn't leave a trace behind.'

Paul was acting. He pretended to half-remember, to half-understand. But his eyes narrowed. Imbecile! Hadn't he been through it all in imagination a hundred times? Hadn't he already been planning and scheming an act for which his brother would reap half the benefit? Nevertheless, he was staggered. He never imagined that the suggestion would come from Henri. He was secretly relieved. If Henri was to receive half the benefit, let him also share half the responsibilities. The risk in any case would be wholly his. He grinned enigmatically, and they put their heads together. And so, in that dim corner of the café was planned the perfect murder.

Coming up against the actual proposition, Paul had long since realized that the affair was not so easy of accomplishment as he had so airily suggested. For the thing must be done without violence, without clues, without a trace. Such ideas as leaving the window open at night were out of the question, as the companion slept in the same room. Moreover, the old lady was quite capable of getting out of bed and shutting it herself if she felt a draught. Some kind of accident? Yes, but what? Suppose she slipped and broke her neck when Paul was in the room. It would be altogether too suspicious. Besides, she would probably only partially break her neck. She would regain sufficient consciousness to tell. To drown her in her bath? The door was always locked or the companion hovering around.

'You've always got to remember,' whispered Paul, 'if any suspicion falls on me, there's the motive. There's strong motive why I should—it's got to be absolutely untraceable. I don't care if some people do suspect afterwards—when we've got the money.'

'What about her food?'

'The food is cooked by Ernestine, and the companion serves it. Besides, suppose I got a chance to tamper with the food, how am I going to get hold of—you know?'

'Weed-killer?'

'Yes, I should be in a pretty position if they traced the fact that I had bought weed-killer. You might buy some and let me have a little on the quiet.'

Henri turned pale. 'No, no; the motive applies to me, too. They'd get us both.'

When the two pleasant gentlemen parted at midnight their plans were still very immature, but they arranged to meet the following evening. It was the thirteenth of the month. To save the situation the deed must be accomplished within eight days. Of course, they wouldn't get the money at once, but, knowing the circumstances, creditors would be willing to wait. When they met the following evening in the Café des Sentiers, Paul appeared flushed and excited, and Henri was pale and on edge. He hadn't slept. He wanted to wash the whole thing out.

'And, sell up your home, I suppose?' sneered Paul.

'Listen, my little cabbage. I've got it. Don't distress yourself. You proposed this last night. I've been thinking about it and watching for months. Ernestine is a good cook, and very methodical. Oh, very methodical! She does everything every day in the same way, exactly to schedule. My apartment is on the same floor, so I am able to appreciate her punctuality and exactness. The old woman eats sparingly and according to routine. One night she has fish. The next night she has a soufflé made with two eggs. Fish, soufflé, fish, soufflé, regular as the beat of a clock. Now, listen. After lunch every day, Ernestine washes up the plates and pans. After that she prepares roughly the evening meal. If it is a fish night, she prepares the fish ready to pop into the pan. If it is a soufflé night, she beats up two eggs and puts them ready in a basin. Having done that, she changes her frock, powders her nose, and goes over to the convent to see her sister who is working there. She is away an hour and a half. She returns punctually at four o'clock. You could set your watch by her movements.'

'Yes, but—'

'It is difficult to insert what I propose in fish, but I don't see any difficulty in dropping it into two beaten-up eggs, and giving an extra twist to the egg-whisk, or whatever they call it.'

Henri's face was quite grey.

'But—but—Paul, how are you going to get hold of the poison?'

'Who said anything about poison?'

'Well, but what?'

'That's where you come in.'

'Yes, you're in it, too, aren't you? You get half the spoils, don't you? Why shouldn't you—some time tomorrow when your wife's out—'

'What?'

'Just grind up a piece of glass.'

'Glass!'

'Yes, you've heard of glass, haven't you? An ordinary piece of broken wine glass will do. Grind it up as fine as a powder, the finer the better, the finer the more effective.'

Henri gasped. No, no, he couldn't do this thing. Very well, then; if he was such a coward, Paul would have to do it himself. And perhaps, when the time came Henri would also be too frightened to draw his dividends. Perhaps, he would like to make them over to his dear brother Paul? Come, it was only a little thing to do. Eight days to the twenty-first. Tomorrow, fish day, but Wednesday would be soufflé. So easy, so untraceable, so safe.

'But you,' whined Henri, 'they will suspect you.'

'Even if they do they can prove nothing. But in order to avoid this unpleasantness, I propose to leave home soon after breakfast. I shall return at a quarter-past three, letting myself in through the stable yard. The stables, as you know, are not used. There is no one else on that floor. Ernestine is upstairs. She only comes down to answer the front door bell. I shall be in and out of the house within five minutes, and I shan't return till late at night, when perhaps—I may be too late to render assistance.'

Henri was terribly agitated. On the one hand was—just murder, a thing he had never connected himself with in his life. On the other hand was comfort for himself and his family, an experience he had given up hoping for. It was in any case not exactly murder on his part. It was Paul's murder. At the same time, knowing all about it, being an accessory before the fact, it would seem contemptible to a degree to put the whole onus on Paul. Grinding up a piece of glass was such a little thing. It couldn't possibly incriminate him. Nobody could ever prove that he'd done it. But it was a terrible step to take.

'Have another cognac, my little cabbage.'

It was Paul's voice that jerked him back to actuality. He said, 'All right, yes, yes,' but whether this referred to the cognac or to the act of grinding up a piece of glass he hardly knew himself.

From that moment to twenty-four hours later, when he handed over a white packet to his brother across the same table at the Café des Sentiers, Henri seemed to be in a nightmarish dream. He had no recollection of how he had passed the time. He seemed to pass from that last cognac to this one, and the interval was a blank.

'Fish today, soufflé tomorrow,' he heard Paul chuckling. 'Brother, you have done your work well.'

When Paul went he wanted to call after him to come back, but he was frightened of the sound of his own voice. He was terribly frightened. He went to bed very late and could not sleep. The next morning he awoke with a headache, and he got his wife to telegraph to the office to say that he was too ill to come. He lay in bed all day, visualizing over and over and over again the possible events of the evening.

Paul would be caught. Someone would catch him actually putting the powder into the eggs. He would be arrested. Paul would give him away. Why did Paul say it was so easy to murder anyone if you lived with them? It wasn't easy at all. The whole thing was chock-a-block with dangers and pitfalls. Pitfalls! At half-past three he started up in bed. He had a vision of himself and Paul being guillotined side by side! He must stop it at any cost. He began to get up. Then he realized that it was already too late. The deed had been done. Paul had said that he would be in and out of the house within five minutes at three-fifteen—a quarter of an hour ago! Where was Paul? Would he be coming to see him? He was going to spend the evening out somewhere, 'returning late at night'.

He dressed feverishly. There was still time. He could call at his aunt's, rush down to the kitchen, seize the basin of beaten-up eggs, and throw them away. But where? How? By the time he got there Ernestine would have returned. She would want to know all about it. The egg mixture would be examined, analysed. God in Heaven! It was too late! The thing would have to go on, and he suffer and wait.

Having dressed, he went out after saying to his wife, 'It's all right. It's going to be all right,' not exactly knowing what he meant. He walked rapidly along the streets with no fixed destination in his mind. He found himself in the Café Rue de la Roquette, where the idea was first conceived, where he had reminded his brother.

He sat there drinking, waiting for the hours to pass.

Soufflé day, and the old lady dined at seven! It was now not quite five. He hoped Paul would turn up. A stranger tried to engage him in conversation. The stranger apparently had some grievance against a railway company. He wanted to tell him all the details about a contract for rivets, over which he had been disappointed. Henri didn't understand a word he was talking about. He didn't listen. He wanted the stranger to drop down dead or vanish into thin air. At last he called the waiter and paid for his reckoning, indicated by a small pile of saucers. From there he walked rapidly to the Café des Sentiers, looking for Paul. He was not there. Six o'clock. One hour more. He could not keep still. He paid and went on again, calling at café after café. A quarter to seven. Pray God that she threw it away. Had he ground it fine enough?

Five minutes to seven. Seven o'clock. Now. He picked up his hat and went again. The brandy had gone to his head. At half-past seven he laughed recklessly. After all, what was the good of life to this old woman of eighty-six? He tried to convince himself that he had done it for the sake of his wife and children. He tried to concentrate on the future, how he could manage on eight or ten thousand francs a year. He would give notice at the office, be rude to people who had been bullying him for years—that old blackguard Mocquin!

At ten o'clock he was drunk, torpid and indifferent. The whole thing was over for good or ill. What did it matter? He terribly wanted to see Paul, but he was too tired to care very much. The irrevocable step had been taken. He went home to bed and fell into a heavy drunken sleep.

'Henri! Henri, wake up! What is the matter with you?' His wife was shaking him. He blinked his way into a partial condition of consciousness. November sunlight was pouring into the room.

'It's late, isn't it?' he said, involuntarily.

'It's past eight. You'll be late at the office. You didn't go yesterday. If you go on like this you'll get the sack, and then what shall we do?'

Slowly the recollection of last night's events came back to him.

'There's nothing to worry about,' he said. 'I'm too ill to go today. Send them another telegram. It'll be all right.'

His wife looked at him searchingly. 'You've been drinking,' she said. 'Oh, you men! God knows what will become of us.'

She appeared to be weeping in her apron. It struck him forcibly at that instant how provoking and small women are. Here was Jeannette crying over her petty troubles. Whereas he—

The whole thing was becoming vivid again. Where was Paul? What had happened? Was it at all likely that he could go down to an office on a day like this, a day that was to decide his fate?

He groaned, and elaborated rather pathetically his imaginary ailments, anything to keep this woman quiet. She left him at last, and he lay there waiting for something to happen. The hours passed. What would be the first intimation? Paul or the gendarmes? Thoughts of the latter stirred him to a state of fevered activity. About midday he arose, dressed, and went out. He told his wife he was going to the office, but he had no intention of doing so. He went and drank coffee at a place up in the Marais. He was terrified of his old haunts. He wandered from place to place, uncertain how to act. Late in the afternoon, he entered a café in the Rue Alibert. At a kiosk outside he bought a late edition of an afternoon newspaper. He sat down, ordered a drink and opened the newspaper. He glanced at the central news page, and as his eye absorbed one paragraph he unconsciously uttered a low scream. The paragraph was as follows:

Mysterious Affair at Chantilly

A mysterious affair occurred at Chantilly this morning. A middle-aged man, named Paul Denoyel, complained of pains in the stomach after eating an omelette. He died soon after in great agony. He was staying with his aunt, Mme Taillandier. No other members of the household were affected. The matter is to be inquired into.

The rest was a dream. He was only vaguely conscious of the events which followed. He wandered through it all, the instinct of self-preservation bidding him hold his tongue in all circumstances. He knew nothing. He had seen nothing. He had a visionary recollection of a plump, weeping Ernestine, at the inquest, enlarging upon the eccentricities of her mistress. A queer woman, who would brook no contradiction. He heard a lot about the fish day and the soufflé day, and how the old lady insisted that this was a fish day and that she had had a soufflé the day before. You could not argue with her when she was like that. And, Ernestine had beaten up the eggs all ready for the soufflé—most provoking! But Ernestine was a good cook, of method and economy. She wasted nothing. What should she do with the eggs? Why, of course, Mr Paul, who since he had come to live there was never content with a *café cornplet*. He must have a breakfast, like these English and other foreigners do. She made him an omelette, which he ate heartily.

Then the beaten-up eggs with their deadly mixture were intended for Mme Taillandier? But who was responsible for this? Ernestine? But there was no motive here. Ernestine gained nothing by her mistress's death. Indeed she only stood to lose her situation. The inquiry went on a long while. Henri himself was conscious of being in the witness box. He knew nothing. He couldn't understand it. His brother would not be likely to do that. He himself was prostrate with grief. He loved his brother.

There was nothing to do but return an open verdict. Shadowy figures passed before his mind's eye—shadowy figures and shadowy realizations. He had perfectly murdered his brother. The whole of the dividends of the estate would one day be his, and his wife's and children's. Eighteen thousand francs a year! One day—

One vision more vivid than the rest—the old lady on the day following the inquest, seated bolt upright at her table, like a figure of perpetuity, playing with the old grey perroquet, stroking its mangy neck.

'There's a pretty lady! Oh, my sweet! Another nice grape for my little one. There's a pretty lady!'